Josie Ross was the quintessential city girl. Haughty. Impatient. Quick-witted and quick-tempered.

Beldon police chief Dan Duvall knew from bitter experience to avoid her type.

So why did he keep thinking about her?

Why did his blood course through his veins like a thoroughbred on a racetrack every time he caught even a glimpse of her? Why did his fingers itch to touch her, to tousle that oh-so-perfect hair? Why did he ache to taste her?

Why did his mind keep creeping back to thoughts of her that could never be repeated aloud in church?

It had to stop.

It just *had* to.

* * *

"Elizabeth Harbison's writing shines with true-to-life characters and in-your-dreams love stories."
   —*USA TODAY* bestselling author Elaine Fox

Dear Reader,

Not only does Special Edition bring you the joys of life, love and family—but we also capitalize on our authors' many talents in storytelling. In our spotlight, Christine Rimmer's exciting new miniseries, VIKING BRIDES, is the epitome of innovative reading. The first book, *The Reluctant Princess,* details the transformation of an everyday woman to glorious royal—with a Viking lover to match! Christine tells us, "For several years, I've dreamed of creating a modern-day country where the ways of the legendary Norsemen would still hold sway. I imagined what fun it would be to match up the most macho of men, the Vikings, with contemporary American heroines. Oh, the culture clash—oh, the lovely potential for lots of romantic fireworks! This dream became VIKING BRIDES." Don't miss this fabulous series!

Our Readers' Ring selection is Judy Duarte's *Almost Perfect,* a darling tale of how good friends fall in love as they join forces to raise two orphaned kids. This one will get you talking! Next, Gina Wilkins delights us with *Faith, Hope and Family,* in which a tormented heroine returns to save her family and faces the man she's always loved. You'll love Elizabeth Harbison's *Midnight Cravings,* in which a sassy publicist and a small-town police chief fall hard for each other and give in to a sizzling attraction.

The Unexpected Wedding Guest, by Patricia McLinn, brings together an unlikely couple who share an unexpected kiss. Newcomer to Special Edition Kate Welsh is no stranger to fresh plot twists, in *Substitute Daddy,* in which a heroine carries her deceased twin's baby and has feelings for the last man on earth she should love—her snooty brother-in-law.

As you can see, we have a story for every reader's taste. Stay tuned next month for six more top picks from Special Edition!

Sincerely,

Karen Taylor Richman
Senior Editor

Please address questions and book requests to:
Silhouette Reader Service
U.S.: 3010 Walden Ave., P.O. Box 1325, Buffalo, NY 14269
Canadian: P.O. Box 609, Fort Erie, Ont. L2A 5X3

Midnight Cravings

ELIZABETH HARBISON

SPECIAL EDITION™

Published by Silhouette Books

America's Publisher of Contemporary Romance

Thanks to the good friends who helped me
whip this book into shape: Annie Jones,
Elaine Fox, Marsha Nuccio and Mary Blayney.
You guys are the best!

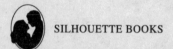 SILHOUETTE BOOKS

ISBN 0-373-24539-4

MIDNIGHT CRAVINGS

Copyright © 2003 by Elizabeth Harbison

Visit Silhouette at www.eHarlequin.com

Printed in U.S.A.

Books by Elizabeth Harbison

Silhouette Special Edition

Drive Me Wild #1476
Midnight Cravings #1539

Silhouette Romance

A Groom for Maggie #1239
Wife without a Past #1258
Two Brothers and a Bride #1286
True Love Ranch #1323
Emma and the Earl #1410
Plain Jane Marries the Boss #1416
Annie and the Prince #1423
His Secret Heir #1528
A Pregnant Proposal #1553
Princess Takes a Holiday #1643

*Cinderella Brides

ELIZABETH HARBISON

has been an avid reader for as long as she can remember. After devouring the Nancy Drew and Trixie Belden series in grade school, she moved on to the suspense of Mary Stewart, Dorothy Eden and Daphne du Maurier, just to name a few. From there it was a natural progression to writing, although early efforts have been securely hidden away in the back of a closet.

After authoring three cookbooks, Elizabeth turned her hand to writing romances and hasn't looked back. Her second book for Silhouette Romance, *Wife without a Past,* was a 1998 finalist for the Romance Writers of America's prestigious RITA® Award in the "Best Traditional Romance" category.

Elizabeth lives in Maryland with her husband, John, daughter Mary Paige, and son Jack, as well as two dogs, Bailey and Zuzu. She loves to hear from readers and you can write to her c/o Box 1636, Germantown, MD 20875.

HUSBAND CONSERVE

1. Select the best man you can find and brush him carefully to rid him of indifference. Be careful not to beat him as you would an egg or cream, for that will make him tough and apt to froth at the mouth.

2. Lift him gently into the home-preserving kettle and tie him with strong cords of affection. Do not sear with sarcasm, for that causes spitting and sputtering, which may result in spontaneous combustion. Scramble when difficulties arise.

3. Do not soak him in liquor. Excessive draughts make him mushy and spongy with your friends, and in the Deep South, stewed husbands have never been popular.

4. Let him simmer at will. Stuff him one hour before taking him out or before asking a great favor of him.

5. Flavor with an oil of happiness, one ounce of understanding and a bushel of fun and laughter.

6. Should he seem weak or troubled with feminine infatuations, smother him in onions and garlic, and treble your charm.

7. Do not spoil him with overindulgence, but serve him daily on a platter of strength and courage, garnished with clean shirts and trousers.

Prologue

In Chief of Police Dan Duvall's view, the annual Rocky Top Chili Cook-off was always a huge pain in the butt.

The problem wasn't just the drunks—although there were plenty of them, thanks to the fact that the contest was sponsored by the local Rocky Top Beer Company—it was the tourists. Everyone in the little town of Beldon, North Carolina (pop. 8,356), sprang to life like citizens of Brigadoon to cater to the visitors. For one long weekend each year, the normally calm residents of the town frantically set up kiosks to sell T-shirts, snacks and four-dollar sodas to all the hot, thirsty, gassy out-of-towners.

"So I'm thinking I'll just sell beans, you know?"

Dan's brother, Jerry, was saying to him as they walked down the shady sidewalk next to Main Street. It was a week before the contest was set to begin and Jerry was, as usual, plotting a get-rich-quick scheme. "Pinto, kidney, green. Because what do people want when they're making chili? *Beans.* I'll make a fortune."

Dan looked at Jerry in disbelief. "This is it? This is the great investment opportunity you had to tell me about?" He looked at the broken-down gazebo old Jeb Currier had offered to lease to Jerry for the week at the "bargain" rate of nine hundred bucks. It was on a small patch of grass off Main Street, right under the old billboard that read Beldon: Home of the Pea Bean. Only some idiot had spray-painted an *r* over the *e* in *Bean,* presumably—and aptly—misspelling *brain.*

"Yup. You could finally get a *safe* job. Hell, you already got shot in the butt in the line of duty...."

"It was my hip," Dan said, with little patience. Eight years ago, Dan had made the mistake of making time with a platinum-blond cook-off contestant from the Deep South. Her chili wasn't so good, but she had other talents. Unfortunately, she also turned out to have a husband, and when he found her with Dan, he did what any gun-toting drunk would do: took one bad shot and passed out.

Jerry didn't know the whole story. He, along with the rest of the town, just knew Dan had been shot by one of the tourists.

"Yeah, whatever," Jerry scoffed. "So, you interested?"

"No." How many times would he have to say it? "I wish everyone would stop thinking of the contest tourists as a gold mine. It's like feeding seagulls at the beach. They'll just keep coming back."

"That's what we *want*." Jerry flipped his hair back out of his eyes. "You're missing the whole point, bro'."

"No, no, that *is* the point. That is *exactly* the point. Every year this town is overrun by bossy, impatient— and sometimes gun-wielding—city folks, and everyone here leaps to serve them. I realize that it's motivated by greed, but with every illegal soda stand, unlicensed T-shirt shop and uninspected *bean gazebo,* the job of every member of my force gets harder. We're talking about six hard-working men and women who end up having to work around the clock, with little or no thanks, every single year for this thing. Don't you get that?"

Jerry looked at him for a moment, then hooked his thumbs into the front pockets of his skintight designer jeans. "I'm going into the bean business, man, and you can join me or not."

Dan looked at Jerry and shook his head. "Get a real job."

"Okay, give one to me. Deputize me."

Dan should have seen this coming. It, too, happened every year. "Not gonna happen, Jer."

"Come on," Jerry whined. "You just said you're shorthanded. I'll do a great job. Give me a chance.

Give me a badge. It's the perfect opportunity for me to get girls.''

"Forget it. If you can't get girls without a badge, you're not gonna get them with one.''

"Easy for you to say,'' Jerry said defensively. "All the chicks go for you.''

Dan held up a hand. "Don't say another word. Not one word.''

"Danny Duvall!'' a voice called behind him.

Dan turned to see the stout figure of Buzz Dewey, president of the Rocky Top Beer Company, approaching as quickly as his short legs could carry his Tweedledum figure. By the time he'd crossed Main Street, he was huffing and puffing.

"Hey, Buzz.'' The man's pallor and physique always made Dan feel like he was a time bomb, ticking down to zero. "Slow down.''

"I'm fine,'' Buzz rasped. "Come on, let's walk. Doc says I need air-obic exercise every day.''

"All right.'' They started walking down Main Street, in the shade of tall pin oak trees and colorful little storefronts. There was Smith's Pharmacy, established in 1925, and Liz Clemens's flower shop and the Beldon Cake Bakery.... It would have been the perfect setting for just about any Frank Capra movie.

"So how are we set for security this year, Danny?''

"Same as always,'' Dan said, stopping in front of the Steak 'n' Eggs so that Buzz didn't overexert himself.

"I ask because it's extra important this year,'' Buzz said, eyeing something behind Dan. Probably the faded photo of a cheeseburger and fries that was taped to the window.

"Why is that?"

Buzz returned his attention to Dan and hiked his brown polyester pants up over his considerable girth until his belt was almost to his armpits. "We've got a celebrity cookbook author, Beatrice Beaujold, coming. Wrote a book on what to cook for men. Spicy things, meaty things, snacks, desserts—what real men like." Buzz looked even hungrier. "Idea being to get 'em to propose marriage, I believe."

"Oh, *that* book." Dan had read an article in the paper about the feminist backlash against the cookbook a few weeks ago.

Buzz nodded. "I get the feeling the author's a real delicate lady-type. I don't want her to be offended by the, uh, *rowdy behavior* of some of our townsfolk during the cook-off."

When a beer company sponsors a chili cook-off, you've got to expect rowdy behavior, Dan thought. The station got calls all night from fussy city folks— no doubt in silk pajamas and slumber masks—complaining about the noise. There was no way he could keep the entire town quiet for one prissy lady.

But Dan couldn't bear to break that news to Buzz, who looked as if one more worry would send him into the coronary he'd been tempting for the past decade or two.

"Take a look at this," Buzz said, taking a rolled-up magazine out of his back pocket. He handed it to Dan. "This is all the protection she's bringing."

There, circled, was a photo of a beautiful, willowy woman with copper hair and a smile as high voltage as anything Dan had ever seen coming out of Hollywood. The caption read ''Page-turner Promotions's newest member, Josephine Ross, at the Zebra Room.''

''She doesn't look like much of a bodyguard,'' Dan said. What she looked like was a whip-smart, sexy city girl. If he didn't know better than to get involved with that kind, he'd probably be putty in her hands. But he did know better. He'd known better since college when he'd made the stupid mistake of handing his heart on a silver platter to a city girl who used it like a rubber ball, bouncing it around until it went flat. It had been flat ever since. Especially where whip-smart, sexy city girls were concerned.

''Exactly! Look at her, can't be more'n twenty-five and if she weighs more than my left leg, I'll eat my hat. If anything, she's going to draw even *more* rowdy attention!''

As if the small police force didn't have enough to deal with. They didn't have the time to serve as private security for the author. In fact, if Dan asked them for any more overtime, he was afraid he was going to get resignations. He'd probably have to take care of this one himself.

''How about this, Buzz?'' he said. ''How about I, personally, keep an extra good eye on your cookbook author?'' That way, at least he could give the other officers a break. Besides, how much attention was one little old cookbook author going to need?

Buzz swabbed a handkerchief across his damp forehead and looked grateful. "That'd be real good of you," he said. "You're a good man, Danny. A good cop. Just like your daddy."

"Well, thanks, Buzz." All of Beldon had thought the world of the late Jack Duvall, whom Dan had replaced as police chief.

"Ms. Beaujold arrives Thursday afternoon," Buzz continued. "If you could be at the Silver Moon Inn, I'd appreciate it."

"I'll be there, don't you worry about a thing," Dan said, resigned. The cook-off was really going to happen. Again.

And something about the picture Buzz had shown him of Josephine Ross made him think this year was going to be even more trouble than usual. He was definitely going to stay out of this woman's way.

Chapter One

SWEET POTATO PUDDING
(from page 14 of *The Way to a Man's Heart*
by Beatrice Beaujold)

Want him to think you're sweet enough to marry?
This one'll do the trick!

4 cups milk
3 cups grated sweet potato
4 eggs, lightly beaten
1 cup sugar
$1/2$ cup flour
2 teaspoons cinnamon
$1/4$ teaspoon nutmeg
$1/4$ cup butter
1 teaspoon salt

Combine everything in a large mixing bowl, then pour it into a casserole dish.

Bake at 350°F for 2 hours, serve, and watch your dreams come true!

Late Thursday afternoon, Josie Ross stood in the lobby of the Silver Moon Inn, cell phone and brief-case in one hand, suitcase in the other, and laptop computer slung over her shoulder, wondering if this was really where she was supposed to be or if some-one at Page-turner Promotions had made a mistake.

She sincerely hoped it wasn't the latter. If someone at the PR firm *had* made a mistake, it was bound to be herself since, at just a couple of months on the job, she was the newest member of the team. Somehow she'd lucked into promoting and assisting Beatrice Beaujold, one of Page-turner's biggest clients and a major cookbook author, this weekend at the Rocky Top Chili Cook-off, so it was absolutely imperative that she make no mistakes.

This job was too important to her to risk losing it because she didn't do right by one of their most im-portant clients.

So she'd done her homework, learning all about the history of the contest, the town and, particularly, the author. She'd asked Beatrice's editor for her impres-sions of the author, along with any special informa-tion Josie might need to know. The editor had com-plied, and that letter had arrived that morning as Josie was leaving. Now it, along with all of her notes and the generous appearance-fee check the brewery had cut for Beatrice, was tucked safely away in her locked briefcase in a large manila envelope marked Beatrice Beaujold.

Josie was *prepared*. It felt good.

With her confidence refreshed, Josie walked through the dark-wood lobby, looking for some sign of either the front desk or Beatrice Beaujold herself.

"Hey, baby," said a dark, bearded man with foam encircling his mouth and a crocheted beer-can hat on his head. He raised a beer mug and sloshed some of the foamy head onto the floor. "Is it hot in here or is it just you?" He gave a lascivious grin and winked.

Josie just kept walking, marveling at how certain types of people—and specifically, the *worst* types of men—could be found anywhere and everywhere. She had a feeling that she would see more of them this weekend than usual.

What would Lyle think if he could see her now? Lyle Bancroft had been Josie's fiancé for nearly five years. He'd left her at the altar the night of their wedding rehearsal. His reasoning, when he could finally be found to give it, was that Josie was too middle-class. Too practical. She wasn't a Bancroft sort of woman. It all added up to the same thing: she wasn't a debutante.

And if Lyle could see her now, in a somewhat shabby inn, surrounded by drunks and the smell of browning onions and chili spice, he would probably feel completely justified in his assessment of her. And, she knew now, he would probably be right.

Josie wandered around for a couple of minutes, unable to find anything that made this look like an inn rather than a frat house. Finally, she stopped a sharp-featured woman with bleached-blond hair and roots as black and gray as half-burned coals. "Excuse me," she said. "Would you happen to know where the check-in desk is?"

"Chicken disk?" the woman repeated with a thick Southern accent. Her teeth were just a little larger than they should have been.

Josie hesitated. "I'm looking for the *check-in* desk." She said it loud and clear, the way one might when speaking to someone whose first language wasn't English. "You know, for my *key.*" She made a key-turning motion in the air.

The woman stared at Josie's hand for a minute, then said in rapid-fire tones, "Yikin gitcher kay oust round there chicken disk, or yonder bind hatthere doorway."

Josie listened with a complete lack of comprehension, leaning forward and straining to pick out even one or two words that she recognized. "Sorry," she said, with an appreciative smile, when the woman ceased making noise. "I didn't quite catch that."

The woman looked exasperated. "I *sayed,* yikin gitcher kay oust round there chicken disk, or yonder bind hatthere doorway." She gestured into the other room as if Josie were an idiot. *"Thar."*

"Ah." Josie nodded as if it had meant something. "I see. Thank you very much." She walked in the direction the woman had indicated, and found herself in a darkened hallway. With a doubtful glance back-

ward, she kept walking and followed the hall around
until it dead-ended in a foyer. From there she followed the sound of voices until she found herself
right back in the room where she'd started, and right
smack in front of the surprised face of the woman
who'd directed her.

Josie gave a quick, polite smile and continued to
follow the crowd to a doorway that had, moments
earlier, been closed, but which was now open to reveal a large and obvious check-in area.

There was also a large display of Beatrice Beaujold's book, *The Way to a Man's Heart: 100 Spicy
Man-Luring Recipes.*

Good. This was the right place.

After making a few minor aesthetic adjustments to
the display, she moved to the end of the check-in line
and took out her PalmPilot to review the weekend's
agenda. Thursday night: Beatrice signs books, talks
with fans. Friday morning: book signing preliminary
round, Beatrice judges. Friday night: free. Saturday:
Beatrice—

"Can I help you, miss?"

Josie jerked her attention back to see a pale wisp
of a brunette behind the desk. She had a faintly fright-
ened look, like a small animal in the shadow of a
large one. "Yes." Josie snapped her PalmPilot shut
and slipped it in her pocket. "Can you tell me if Beatrice Beaujold has checked in yet?"

"I don't know," the girl answered vaguely.

Her accent was light and Josie could understand
her without any trouble, but when she didn't say any-

thing further, Josie wondered if the girl had trouble understanding her.

"It's Beaujold," she said. "B-E-A-U-J-O-L-D." Silence. "Could you check, please?"

"Why, yes, yes, I could."

Josie waited again while the girl did nothing. "*Would* you?" she asked finally, realizing that this game was all about picking the right words.

"Certainly," the girl responded, and looked at the computer screen before her. "No, she hasn't arrived yet." She nodded very seriously. "That's what I thought."

"Thanks for looking," Josie said with some irritation. She set her bags down and took her wallet out of her purse. "I guess I'll just go ahead and check in myself."

Blank stare.

"My name's Josephine Ross." She gestured toward the computer. "I think you'll find I'm in the room adjoining Ms. Beaujold's suite. In fact, since I reserved both rooms, I may as well do the check-in for both now. I'll give Ms. Beaujold her key when she comes in." It was one small thing she could do to make things a little easier for Beatrice when she arrived. Josie took her brand-new company credit card out, set it on the counter and stepped back to wait. The smell of beer hung in the air like mist.

The girl took the card, ran it through the slider, then tapped at the computer with one finger. It took her about ten minutes, but she finally looked up and announced, "This card's been declined."

"What?" Josie's jaw dropped.

"It was declined." The girl started to take a pair of scissors out of the drawer.

"Whoa, wait a minute!" Josie snatched the card from the girl. "There must be some kind of mistake. I'll call the company. Meanwhile, just use this one." She foraged in her purse for her personal credit card and prayed there was enough room on it to cover expenses. Her savings had dipped very, very low while she was looking for a job. Page-turner had hired her just in the nick of time.

She waited uncomfortably for about five minutes until the girl handed the card back to her, along with a carbon slip for her signature. "I've signed you in. I'll just get your keys." Remarkably, she turned to do so without being specifically asked.

When she got the large brass keys, Josie thanked the girl, picked up her case and stepped away from the counter so the next poor guest could try their luck with her. Slipping the keys into her pocket, she took the company credit card back out of her purse and opened her cell phone so she could find out what the problem was.

Unfortunately, the phone registered that it couldn't find a signal. She moved around the room, then out onto the deck, hauling her luggage along with her and watching the face of the phone for some sign of life.

"It's no use, there's no cell tower around here," a kind-faced woman with bright blue eyes and apple cheeks said to Josie.

Josie felt like a foreigner abroad upon spotting an American compatriot. "You already tried?"

The woman smiled and took a similar phone out of her purse. "I've been trying since ten miles outside of Charlotte."

"Well." Josie put the phone away. "I guess I can do without it for a few days. Somehow." She'd just use her card and fill out an expense report when she got back. She set her heavy bags down and held out her hand. "Josie Ross."

The woman took it and smiled. "Dolores Singer. But you can call me Buffy." She must have taken a lot of flack for her nickname in the past because before Josie could respond, she held up a hand and said, "Yes, seriously. To my great misfortune, I was a fan of *Family Affair* as a child and my father started calling me Buffy. Before I knew what hit me, it stuck. He meant well."

"I loved that show." Josie laughed, remembering that she even had a Mrs. Beasley doll once. "So, I'm guessing from your accent that you're not from these parts."

"Nope. Cleveland. How about you?"

"Manhattan. It feels like another planet."

"I know what you mean," Buffy agreed. "I like it. It's so laid-back here. Very relaxing."

Josie thought that *forced* relaxation was anything but relaxing, but she didn't say it. "So, are you here for the chili cook-off? Representing Ohio with some Cincinnati-style chili, perhaps?"

Buffy shook her head. "Actually, I came to meet

Beatrice Beaujold. She's the one who wrote the man-luring cookbook. I owe her a huge debt of gratitude.''

"You do? Why?"

"It's thanks to her that I'm engaged to be married.''

"Really?" Josie asked, ever a sucker for romance, as long as it wasn't close enough to break *her* heart. "Because of her recipes?"

"I think so." Buffy blushed. "He actually fell to his knees two bites into her sweet potato pudding at a Memorial Day picnic." She shrugged. "All I can think is that it had something to do with the recipe because I sure didn't see it coming."

Josie was extremely skeptical, but she knew it was her job to foster this idea, not to discourage it. Rather than lie, she just remained silent.

"I know it sounds crazy, but I guess crazier things have happened."

Josie smiled. "Congratulations. I hope you'll be very happy." She glanced at her watch. "It's been nice chatting with you, but I need to go to my room to use the phone."

"The rooms here don't have phones."

"What?"

"No phones in the rooms."

Josie closed her eyes for a moment and took a deep breath. "So I'm guessing fax machines are out of the question."

"Afraid so." Buffy gave an understanding smile. "It's a little bit of a time warp, but I think it adds to the peaceful atmosphere."

Josie sighed. This was *not* making her feel peaceful.

"Try the little hall just inside the front door," Buffy suggested. "I think I saw a pay phone there."

Josie thanked her and carried her things back into the hallway Buffy had described and set her heavy suitcase down. Sure enough, there was a pay phone, but it was about a hundred years old and the reception crackled like lightning before she even pressed zero for the operator. She fidgeted with the wire, trying to find a position in which the line was quiet enough to make a call, but it didn't work.

Exasperated, she muttered an oath about tiny backward towns and put the phone down. God willing, there would be a working phone in her room. She'd go on up and make her call quickly so she didn't miss Beatrice's arrival. Satisfied with her plan, she went to pick up her suitcase.

It was gone.

How on earth had someone taken her suitcase? She had not been more than three feet away from it, and there was no one else around. How could someone have slipped in, taken the case and run off with it without her hearing a thing, all in the span of about a minute and a half?

She looked around, thinking someone must have moved it for some reason. It was no place obvious. She ran upstairs to check Beatrice's room and her own, where she left the rest of her things. When she came back downstairs, she asked the girl at the check-in desk if someone who worked there had taken it to a back room, but she was only met with a blank stare and a contention that "We don't have a back room for suitcases."

"Is there a manager on duty?" Josie asked the girl, trying valiantly to keep her voice courteous even though she wanted to scream at the girl to *wake up*.

"There's the owner. I *guess* you'd call her a manager."

"Good," Josie said, trying to take control of the situation. She thought of the check for Beatrice. The letter from her editor. "Would you please ask her to come speak with me?" she asked, her voice rising. "Maybe she can help me get this sorted out."

"Okay." Smile. Nod.

Every muscle in Josie's body tensed. "Could you do it now?"

"Oh. Okay." She disappeared into a room behind the desk, and Josie took another look around the lobby. She covered the whole thing, everywhere she'd been. It was nowhere. She was about to go outside and check the wide wraparound front porch, when she was interrupted by a gentle Southern voice, like that of a character in *Gone With the Wind*.

"Excuse me, Ms. Ross?"

She turned to see a woman standing at the counter who looked like she was playing a Southern dame in a movie, her fingertips touching the forearm of one of the most shockingly handsome men Josie had ever seen.

"Ms. Ross, I'm Myrtle Fairfield and this is Dan Duvall," the woman said, in that quiet, sweet voice steel magnolias tended to have. "He's with the police. I understand you've had a little problem with your suitcase. Mr. Duvall is here to help."

She wouldn't have pegged him as a policeman. He looked more like a movie star. He was tall, with wavy dark hair and clear eyes the blue of a summer sky. Faint lines fanned out from the corners, giving him the pleasant expression of a man who smiled a lot.

"Thanks for your concern, Officer," Josie said, all too aware that she hadn't had the chance to go to her room and freshen up since the two-hour flight and three-hour drive here this morning. Alarm bells went off in her head, giving her the foolish impulse to primp and make herself more presentable for this Adonis, even as she realized that she shouldn't care what he thought of her personally. She wasn't only irritated by her reaction to him, she was surprised by it. It had been ages since she'd felt that stir in her chest, but this kind of guy—one so gorgeous you just *knew* he had a stable of women to choose from—was *not* the kind of guy she wanted to start thinking romantic thoughts about.

He smiled, showing even white teeth and a dent that could almost be called a dimple. "Call me Dan," he said. "Please."

She swallowed. Hard. "All right, Dan."

He took a step closer to her. He smelled good. Like Ivory soap and clean clothes. Somehow Josie found that reassuring.

"So your bag was stolen," he said. "Were you hurt in the attack?"

"No, no, there was no attack." She tried to will her pounding heart to calm down. "I wasn't there."

"You weren't there."

"No. Well, yes." He had her flustered. This was bad. "I mean, I was just a couple of feet away. See, I set it down for a moment while I tried to make a call at the pay phone off the lobby. The phone didn't work, so it couldn't have been longer than a minute or so, but when I hung up, it was gone." She tossed an apologetic look to Myrtle. "I'm sorry to trouble you with this. I'm sure there's a logical explanation." *Please, please, please let there be a logical explanation,* she prayed, returning her thoughts to the more important problem at hand.

"It's no trouble," Myrtle answered, but she looked very troubled.

"You say you left it over there?" Dan asked, indicating the hallway, where now there was a small crowd of people, apparently having a contest to see who could toss the most peanuts in the air and catch them in their mouths.

"Yes," Josie said. "Right there where all the peanuts are on the floor now."

Dan Duvall's voice grew about one hundred and five percent less sympathetic than it had been when he'd first walked over. "And you weren't keeping an eye on it?"

She swallowed a terse retort. "I got a little distracted for just a minute. But, as I said, I was only a couple of feet away."

"You shouldn't have left your things unattended. Anyone could come along and pick 'em up.''

"That seems obvious now.''

"Did you see anyone suspicious hanging around?'' Myrtle asked, kneading her crepey hands.

"I'll get the details,'' Dan said, patting the older woman's thin shoulder. "It looks like Lily Rose needs some help at the counter now.'' He gestured toward the girl at the check-in counter, who was now looking fretful and fluttering her hands like birds in front of her as she tried to help an increasingly long line of impatient guests.

Myrtle gave an exclamation and bustled over to help poor Lily Rose, muttering about beer drinkers.

Dan Duvall smiled after her, then turned back to Josie, his smile disappearing, and asked for a description of the missing items.

She gave it to him, noticing that he didn't bother to write any of it down. "There was an envelope in the side pocket that was clearly marked with the name Beatrice Beaujold,'' she explained. "It occurred to me that maybe someone at the hotel had taken it up to Beatrice's room, thinking it was hers, but it wasn't there when I looked.''

"What was in the envelope?''

"Nothing very interesting to anyone but me. Beatrice's bio and picture, and some flyers and information about this contest. My own notes.'' She took a short breath. "A check for Beatrice. Her appearance fee from the brewery.''

"Well, it's not like someone else could endorse it and cash it."

"Maybe not, but she's expecting to pick it up when she gets here."

"I understand. You didn't lose any cash?"

"No." She tried to sound calm.

"Well, that's good. I'm afraid I'm not sure how much we can do to help you," he said, looking as if he didn't want to do anything at all to help. "But we'll certainly be on the lookout."

There was the sound of smashing glass in the corner and Dan Duvall's eyes jerked to the scene. His mouth went tight.

"'S'all right," someone called, waving a feeble hand. "'N'accident."

A muscle ticked in Dan's jaw.

Josie tried to get his attention back. "Do you want me to write the description down?" she asked, trying to sound helpful although she was annoyed at how little concern he was showing for her loss. "So you don't forget?"

"That won't be necessary. We'll let you know if it turns up." He gave a short nod and turned to go.

"Wait a minute."

He turned back, his face a mask of patience. "Ma'am?"

"What am I supposed to do now?"

He raised an eyebrow, apparently waiting for her to elaborate.

"I mean, that stuff is really important to me, even though it isn't particularly interesting to anyone else.

I need it back.'' She thought of the letter Beatrice's editor, Susan Pringle, had written. She'd barely had a moment to glance at it, but the first paragraph had mentioned there were some ''special challenges'' when handling Beatrice in public. It had also said that there was some ''confidential material'' in the letter and that Josie should be careful not to let it go astray, but before Josie had been able to read further, her flight had been announced and she'd put the letter away.

She'd intended to read it on the plane, but the flight had been turbulent, and as soon as she'd gotten off the plane, she'd had to drive a car, and…well, she just hadn't gotten to read the note.

At the time it had seemed so offhand it hadn't occurred to Josie that it was any more important or confidential than any personnel file. Now her mind reeled with imagined possibilities.

''I *really* need my briefcase back,'' she emphasized. ''Should I go to the police station and fill out an official report?''

''You could,'' he said, a hint of slow molasses in his accent. ''But there's really no point.''

''It would make me feel better to know it was properly reported.''

''You're reporting it now.''

''I am,'' she said, trying to keep from gritting her teeth. ''But are you?''

He gave a maddeningly lazy smile. ''Why, yes, ma'am. I am. I don't have time to go into the station to take your report right this minute, but I'll file it as soon as I can."

She narrowed her eyes at him, suspecting he was patronizing her. "Look, there were some really important papers in that envelope. I'd feel better seeing someone commit this report to black and white right now." Though she thought better of it an instant later, she couldn't resist adding, "The way most police would."

"I see."

"So where is the station house?"

"Corner of Elm and Magnolia. But we're really shorthanded. If you go in they'll just have you wait until the chief of police gets in and that's—"

"Good," she said, her voice tense. "I'm eager to speak with him."

He smiled again. Not a friendly smile, but an amused one. On a different person, under different circumstances, it might have been boyish, mischievous. "I've got a feeling you may change your mind about that," he said.

"I won't." She gave a polite smile and turned to leave the room. A minute later, she stepped into the muggy sunshine and walked purposefully out to the street. God knew where she was going to go once she got there, but she had the feeling that Dan might be watching her, smugly assuming she'd get lost, and she didn't want to give him the satisfaction of seeing her standing on the sidewalk wringing her hands and trying to figure out which way to go.

Luck was on her side. As soon as she reached the

sidewalk she saw that the sign on the nearest cross street indicated it was Elm. So she kept on walking, as if she'd lived here all her life and knew just where to go.

When she was safely out of sight of the inn, she slowed her pace and looked around. The street was about twice as wide as the little suburban street she'd grown up on, and it was lined with tall, shady oaks. Enormous Victorian mansions faced out, looking for all the world as if they had been drawn by Walt Disney. As a matter of fact, the people looked like that, too. A couple of older women stood on either side of a garden fence, each wearing floppy hats and gardening gloves, talking and smiling and nodding to Josie as she passed.

It was hard to reconcile the fact that she'd been robbed, since she felt so completely safe walking through the streets alone. It was a feeling she wasn't entirely familiar with, since part of her was always on alert when she walked in the city.

By contrast, the pace was so leisurely in this town that Josie actually felt as if her own heart rate had slowed to about half its usual pace, despite the urgency of getting her things back. *Why bother to pound any faster?* it probably thought. *There's nothing in Beldon to get excited about.*

Where the houses stopped, a large, verdant stretch of woods started. In Manhattan, this kind of change signaled dangerous isolation, but in Beldon it was just a pleasant break before a lovely little row of storefronts with apartments over them. The shops all had elaborate colonial facades and were painted in vivid colors. The quaintness was so uniform that Josie wondered if there was a penalty for having a plain building.

That question was answered, though, when she got to the police station. It was a redbrick box, with nothing to distinguish it except a cement sign over the door that read, in block letters, Police Station.

Josie took a short, bolstering breath and opened the creaking wooden door to go inside. There were three empty desks, a single bookshelf with volumes with titles such as *Beldon Police Report, April '72—August '73,* and a plain, round clock with black hands that told her it had taken approximately seven minutes for her to walk there from the inn.

This was one small town.

"Hello?" Josie called out. "Is anyone here?"

There was a startled exclamation and the clanging of metal before a man called, "Hello? Who's there?"

"No one you know," Josie answered. "Just a visitor to the town. I'm looking for the chief of police."

"Er, he's not in."

"Who are you?"

Long pause. "I'm...uh...Deputy Fife...er. No, Deputy Pfeiffer."

"Well, could you come out and talk to me, Deputy Pfeiffer? I have a robbery to report."

"Don't sound like you're from around here."

"I'm not. Do I have to be from here to report a crime?" she asked, annoyed. What was it going to take to get someone to act responsibly around here? Or just to *act?*

"I'm a little…indisposed."

She counted to five before saying, "Look, Deputy, I'm sure you're very busy, but would it kill you to come out and have a word with me?"

A moment passed before he said, "I can't."

"Why not?"

Another moment passed. "I'm locked in."

"What?" She didn't even bother to hide her astonishment.

"Well, uh, I was cleaning one of the cells and I let the door shut behind me." A beat passed. "Can you let me out?"

"How?" Amazing. As if she didn't already have enough to handle, now she had to free the police from jail. It was incredible. This was like a bad sitcom.

"I, uh, left the keys in there on the wall."

She looked around at the walls. There was nothing on them except the clock, some FBI Wanted posters that looked to be several years old, and a Vargas Girl calendar that was, on closer inspection, from 1959. "I don't see any keys hanging on the wall," she called.

"Must have left them in my desk, then," the voice returned. "See the desk by the door? One with the pinup-girls calendar?"

"Yes."

"Try the top drawer."

She couldn't believe she had to release the deputy from a jail cell before she could report her stolen bags. How in the world did she end up in this ridiculous town? Why wasn't it rife with criminals, since the police were so inept?

If she weren't an honest person she'd consider robbing a bank right about now.

In fact, if things with Page-turner didn't work out after this weekend, she'd keep it in mind, she thought wryly.

"I'm looking," she said, opening the drawer. There were some pens and pencils, a couple of paper clips bent out of shape, a pack of cinnamon gum, a set of handcuffs and a cracked black-and-white photo of a handsome young man in a police uniform, flanked by what appeared to be his proud parents.

Josie lingered on the picture for a moment, wondering who the man was and what his story was, then set it down.

"Find them?" the voice called from the back.

"Not yet."

"Look in the back of the drawer."

She pulled it out as far as it would go, then reached in. Sure enough, she snagged a set of keys on a large brass ring. "I think I found them," she said, slamming the drawer shut just as the front door creaked open and Dan Duvall came in.

"Officer Duvall," she said in a clipped voice, closing her hand around the cold set of keys. "I thought you were too busy to come into the station."

For a moment he didn't speak. He looked at her, then at the key ring in her hand. Then he asked, "What the hell are you doing going through my desk?"

Chapter Two

CHOCOLATE PUDDING
(from page 86 of *The Way to a Man's Heart*
by Beatrice Beaujold)

Chocolate makes you feel like you're in love...or in
lust. The better the chocolate, the better the lust....

1 cup sugar
1/4 cup cornstarch
1/2 teaspoon salt
1/4 teaspoon pure chili powder
8 oz. bitter chocolate, chopped
2 egg yolks
2 2/3 cups milk
2 tablespoons butter
2 teaspoons vanilla

In a heavy saucepan, whisk together sugar, cornstarch, salt and chili powder. Then add chocolate.

Whisk egg yolks and milk together and gradually whisk into chocolate mixture. Bring mixture just to a boil over moderate heat, whisking constantly, and boil 1 minute, whisking. Remove pan from heat and whisk in butter and vanilla.

Divide pudding between 6 ramekins or small custard bowls. Chill and serve.

"*Your* desk?" Josie asked, looking around at the other desks. "I didn't go through your desk."

In the back, there was the faint sound of Deputy Pfeiffer clearing his throat.

Dan strode over to Josie and took the key ring from her hand. "*My* keys," he said, in a low, controlled voice, "were in *my* desk." He thumped his hand on the desk in front of her. "So I repeat, what the hell do you think you're doing?"

She stood up and put her hands on her hips. "Deputy Pfeiffer—" whom she dearly hoped outranked Dan Duvall "—locked himself in a cell back there and asked me to get his keys for him so he could get out. I'm doing just that."

Dan looked incredulous. "*Deputy Pfeiffer?*"

She felt her face grow warm, even though she hadn't done anything wrong. "Yes, Deputy Pfeiffer," she said, gesturing toward the open doorway in the back. "He locked himself in and asked me to get the keys for him."

"Oh, I'll bet he did," Dan said, shaking his head. Then he laughed. He actually *laughed*.

At her.

"Just what's so funny?"

"Usually, people like you are begging me to lock the troublemakers up, they're not coming in and springing them."

"I'm not *springing* anyone. I came in here to file a proper report and I found your deputy locked in."

A long moment stretched thin in silence while he looked at her in a way that made her skin tingle from head to toe.

"Honey, I don't even *have* a deputy."

Horrible realization came over her like a bucket of cold water. "Oh, my God."

He shook his head. "Didn't you think it was a little strange that the deputy was locked up in a cell?"

"Yes, of course." It was hard to defend what was, in retrospect, such an idiotic action, but she tried. "But so far the police department has been so efficiency-challenged that nothing about it could surprise me."

"Well, we keep the criminals locked up here in Beldon. What do they do with them where you come from?"

She pressed her lips together for a moment. "All right, I get it. Who is he really?"

Without averting his eyes from hers, he called, "Tell her your real name, Deputy."

After a moment, the voice answered, "Henry Lawtell."

"What are you in for?"

"No good reason!"

Still holding her gaze, Dan said, "Henry's in jail for the third time this year after drinking a trough of beer and riding his motorcycle into the statue of Alexander Beldon in the town center. Naked."

"Oh."

The corners of his mouth twitched as if he was trying not to smile. "Didn't the name Deputy Pfeiffer sound familiar to you?"

Deputy Pfeiffer. Deputy Fife. Of course it did, she just hadn't made the connection. Suddenly, it seemed painfully obvious. Humiliation burned in her cheeks, made worse by the fact that she knew he could see it.

"You all right, Ms. Ross?" He stood up and made a show of ushering her into his chair. "You look a little flushed. Guess you're not used to the heat down here."

"I'm fine." She shrugged her arm out of his warm grasp. "We have heat in New York."

He gave her a long gaze, which made her wonder if it was an offense to snap at a police officer in this town. She wasn't thrilled at the prospect of playing out her own Mayberry *Midnight Express*.

"Different kind of heat," he said.

"Bring her back here so I can get a look at her," Henry called from his jail cell. "She sounds real cute."

"Oh, she is," Dan drawled, looking her over so brazenly that she felt as if she'd been touched.

But she didn't want to be touched, she reminded herself. She had a lot of troubles to deal with right now; she *definitely* didn't need to add a man to the mix. She already knew she didn't have good luck with men—there was no point in even trying.

Too bad her body didn't agree with her mind on that. Every time she looked at Dan, her pulse quickened and her nerves sprang to life. Even now, the flush in her cheeks flamed so hot she thought her eyelashes might get singed.

''But she's a pain in the ass,'' he added.

Josie stood tall, hoping he didn't notice her agitation. ''This is hardly professional behavior, *Officer*.''

''No?''

''Certainly not.''

''Sweetheart, if I were to behave professionally, I'd have slapped the cuffs on you the minute I walked in and saw you going through my desk and stealing my keys in order to release a prisoner.'' One side of his mouth curled into a smile. ''That what you want?''

Suddenly, she had the distinct impression that those handcuffs had seen less criminal action than personal. Her face went hot again.

She swallowed hard. ''No, thank you. And for your information, if I had gone back there and seen that man wasn't in uniform, I would *not* have let him out.''

''I'm glad to hear it.''

Satisfied that she'd redeemed herself at least a little, she said, ''I'd like to speak with your supervisor now, please.''

"What's she look like, Danny?" Henry called from the back.

Josie and Dan exchanged glances, each challenging the other.

"She looks pissed," Dan said.

"No, I mean, like, what color hair does she have?"

"'Bout the color of that dark lager you pickled yourself in the other night." Judging by the way he looked at her, for a moment Josie thought he might reach out and touch her. "What do you call that color?" he asked, with the kind of cocky pirate smile that Josie sometimes, on the right person, found irresistible.

"Does your chief approve of you talking to people this way when they come in for help?"

"He approves of everything I do."

The mental list she was making of his offenses was growing by the second. By the time she was finished talking with his boss, she wouldn't be surprised—or sorry—if he was fired on the spot. "We'll see about that. You do realize I'm here to see the chief, right? I assume he's not locked in a cell or bound and gagged in a closet."

"Nope. Around here, you can tell the police by the fact that they're *not* locked up."

"That seems to be the only distinction," she said. "Can you call him on your radio and get him here?"

"No need to do that, he's here."

She looked around toward the door, expecting to see a kindly gray-haired man who could save her from the unsavory scrutiny of Dan Duvall. Although if he was here, why on earth hadn't he stepped in earlier? "Where?"

"Right here." He splayed his arms wide and smiled even wider.

She felt it coming a split second before he said it.

"I'm the police chief."

Josie's stomach felt like a popped balloon. "Of course you are," she said, more to herself than to him. "I've seen this movie before."

Dan laughed. "You wanted to talk to me about something? The insubordination of one of my men, I believe?"

"That's very funny. Who's your boss, Chief?" She reached into her purse and took out her PalmPilot. "I'd like the name, number and address, please."

"That'd be the mayor. You can find him at City Hall."

"Fine."

"But I don't think you're gonna like him as much as you like me."

"Meaning...?"

"I'm your best hope for satisfaction here."

Her breath caught in her throat. "What the—"

"In the matter of your stolen property, that is." He looked at her as if he couldn't possibly have meant anything else. "Now, as I told you before, we're doing all we can to get your suitcase back, but it might just take some time. You can come on into the station every day and file more reports, but all that's gonna do is keep us from getting out to where we might find your things."

"I don't get the impression that you're out looking for my things, anyway." She put the idea of him satisfying her out of her mind as best she could.

"I don't know what else you want me to do. Send an APB out to the state police? If someone stole your suitcase, they've probably either hidden it away in their room—in which case, we can't search every room—or they've rifled through it and tossed it somewhere outside, in which case we'll come across it any time now."

"Or maybe they're wandering around with it right now, or shoving it into the car trunk so they can get away with it."

He laughed. "I'll keep an eye out for that, too."

It was hopeless. She may as well just go shopping for new clothes, because she was never going to see her old ones again. She'd also have to find a fax machine somewhere in this town and hope that someone in the office had copies of everything except the letter to fax to her.

But before she did anything else, she had to contact the brewery and ask them to cut another check for Beatrice.

"Thanks for your help, Chief." Josie was unable to keep the edge off her tone. "You certainly know how to make a girl feel safe." She turned to go but was stopped by a strong hand on her upper arm.

He turned her to face him and his expression was serious. "You're safe, Ms. Ross. Don't doubt that."

For just a moment, she didn't. He was tall and strong and obviously capable, at least in a physical sense. It had been so long since she'd had someone to lean on that, for just one insane moment, she would have liked to fall into the cloak of his arms and let the whole outside world disappear.

She shook herself out of the thought immediately. "Thanks. But at this point, I would settle for simply being *dressed* this weekend."

His gaze swept over her like wind. "Look dressed to me."

Funny, for a moment there, she didn't *feel* dressed. "This is the only outfit I have now," she said, swallowing the disconcerting sexual awareness of him that she felt. "My clothes, my shampoo, my toothbrush, everything was in that suitcase."

Dan's expression softened. "Listen, I don't mean to seem insensitive, but there's *always* trouble during this contest. The odds of finding a stolen suitcase, with everything else that's going on, are pretty low. Thieves in this situation tend to do one of two things, as I told you. They either hide the item away, so it can't be found, or they take what they want and toss the rest. If it's the latter, we'll find it. Otherwise, don't hold your breath."

"Nice little town you've got here."

"Believe it or not, normally Beldon *is* a nice place. Maybe not the kind of place you city folks would want to hang out in, but a nice, quiet place. However, during this cook-off, things are a little different. Every year, for this one weekend, the whole town becomes a bar."

She softened. "I'm sure that's a nightmare for you,

but I don't get the feeling you're concerned about my stolen property at all.''

"I am. You'll just have to trust me on this.''

She looked into his eyes, wondering how many gullible women had heard that very line.

She swallowed hard. "I'd appreciate whatever you can do.''

He smiled. "That's more like it. Around here we take things more slowly.''

"I fully appreciate that you do things differently around here,'' she said, her voice tight. She was off to a *terrible* start this weekend. "But I'm only here for four days and I don't have the luxury of taking things slowly.''

She thought again of the missing envelope, with the letter about Beatrice. It wasn't as if she could call the editor, tell her the letter had been lost and ask if she could send another copy. Beatrice's publisher was a major client of Page-turner Promotions and Josie absolutely couldn't afford to risk alienating the publisher, for fear that they would drop her company altogether. And that the company, in turn, would drop her.

On top of that, Josie thought with horror, what if the confidential information was sensitive in the sense that the public shouldn't get wind of it? Beatrice was the celebrity author of the moment, and a lot of journalists were trying to tear her down. On top of that, thanks to the theme of her cookbook, Beatrice had come under the feminists' wrath, so that was another whole group looking for ammo against her.

But Josie couldn't let Dan Duvall know all of that. Who knew what motivated him? "Look," she said, "I really need some of the papers that were stolen. For work. They're not of interest to anyone else, but if you find anything that looks like it could be relevant, you would save me an awful lot of hassle."

He shrugged. His shoulders were really quite broad under the thin cotton of his shirt. If he *wanted* to catch criminals, he probably could, bare-handed. "You got it. Well, it was nice meeting you, Miss Ross."

"Ms.," she corrected automatically, then immediately regretted it.

"Ms.," he amended, showing the almost-dimple. "My apologies." He was dismissing her, there was no doubt about it.

She hesitated. Dismissive or not, he was obviously trying. He didn't know how important those stolen papers were to her. "I'm sorry about the desk. And—" she gestured "—Deputy Pfeiffer back there. Although, as I said, I wouldn't have let him out."

A little warmth came into his eyes and they crinkled at the corners. He was a great-looking man. In fact, he would be a deadly combination for some women. "It's like I always say, you city folks are just too trusting."

"We are, huh?" She couldn't help but smile, albeit reluctantly.

Incredibly, he smiled back. "Oh, yeah."

A tremor coursed through Josie.

Suddenly there was a loud ruckus at the door. A man who looked like a thin, wiry version of Dan Duvall was led in, apparently against his will, by two older gentlemen.

"I didn't know it was a wig!" the dark-haired man was protesting loudly.

Dan sighed. "Excuse me," he said to Josie, and got up from his desk.

Although she was curious about what was going on, the office was so small that there was no way she could stand by unobtrusively and watch. "Please call me at the inn when you've found my things," she said. "I'm in room 508."

"I know where you are."

Josie watched as he strode across the room. He moved well, she noticed. Not many men could look graceful and masculine at the same time. It was hard to take her eyes off of him, but she managed, then left.

Dan Duvall did have his hands full, Josie had to admit. Maybe she should have been more patient with him. How many thousands of times had her mother repeated the cliché about catching flies with honey instead of vinegar?

She also had Beatrice to consider. It wouldn't be good for Beatrice's public image to have her publicist arguing with the chief of police.

Which reminded her, Beatrice must surely have made it to the Silver Moon Inn by now. It was after seven o'clock.

She hurried back through the town, barely noticing the many picture-postcard scenes, to the inn. After a ten-minute search of the lobby and upstairs rooms,

Josie feared that Beatrice not only wasn't there, but she might not be coming at all.

No sooner did she have the thought than the front doors banged open. A round elderly woman, with gray curls atop her apple-cheeked visage, made her way in, using a knotted cane for support. Behind her was a young woman, with lank dark hair and a figure like a toothpick, holding a baby.

It was Beatrice. It had to be. Josie let out a long pent-up breath and thanked God that things were *finally* going to get back on track.

Her thanks went out just a moment too soon.

"Get the hell out of my way, boy, I don't need your damn help!"

Josie stopped short and watched in open-mouthed horror as Beatrice Beaujold whacked the bellboy in the shins with her cane.

That's not Beatrice, Josie thought as the woman raised her cane again and thumped it against the hapless bellboy's leg. *That can't be her.*

But it was her, all right. Josie recognized her from her publicity photos.

Something must have happened that Josie didn't see, something to justify Beatrice's outburst. Maybe the bellboy had touched her accidentally, she reasoned. And Beatrice thought he was being fresh.

Josie didn't quite believe it, but no better explanation was coming to her. There had to be a good reason for what must surely be a rare outburst. Beatrice Beaujold was kind, a grandmother figure, the sort of wise older woman people went to for advice.

That was the image her colleagues at Page-turner Promotions had projected for her.

Obviously, she'd just been caught at a bad moment. Josie would have a delicate word with her about publicity and how important it was to maintain a good public image.

She steeled herself and crossed the lobby to where the older woman was still creating a commotion.

"Ms. Beaujold?" Josie said as she drew near.

"Who's that?" Beatrice snapped, squinting behind thick round glasses.

Josie extended her hand. "I'm Josie Ross, from Page-turner Promotions. We spoke on the phone."

"Oh, yeah?" Beatrice looked Josie up and down, as if she were assessing a prize on *Let's Make a Deal*.

From the look on her face, Josie expected her to either bid a dollar or ask for the goat behind door number three.

"That all you're wearing?" Beatrice asked.

"W-what?" Josie stammered, putting a hand to her sleeveless silk blouse. "What I'm *wearing?*"

"Hardly decent." Beatrice sniffed and lowered her voice to a stage whisper. "Go cover yourself, girlie. No one needs to see all that bare flesh."

Josie glanced at her knee-length skirt and sleeveless white blouse, which she was evidently going to be wearing all weekend unless she could find a decent clothing store, and wondered what Beatrice was seeing that she was not. "I'm sorry, I don't under—"

"A little modesty never hurt," Beatrice declared.

There was no answer to that. Josie decided her best

bet was to change the subject. "Well. Is this your niece, Ms. Beaujold?" she asked, smiling at the girl with the baby.

Beatrice shot a glance at the young woman with the baby. "Yes. Cher, introduce yourself proper, girl."

The girl lurched to attention, as much as her stick figure and the chubby baby in her arms would allow. "I'm Cher," she said dully.

Beatrice rolled her eyes. "Baby's Britney, if you can believe that. My brother's kin." She widened her eyes, shook her head and all but cranked her index finger in a circle at her temple.

Josie forced a smile. This was no momentary lapse, she realized with horrible certainty. This was Beatrice's personality. No wonder no one else wanted to take on this job.

No wonder Susan Pringle had written confidentially about "special challenges" with Beatrice. God knew what that letter said, but if it got out…. At best, the public would get wind of some less-than-flattering comments about Beatrice. At worst, Beatrice would get wind of them herself and leave her publisher. Who might then fire Page-turner.

Who would then almost certainly fire Josie.

It didn't bear thinking about.

"And are they staying for the evening?" Josie asked in a voice not quite her own.

"Weekend," Beatrice corrected. "I'm stuck with 'em." She gave Josie a look that challenged her to have a complaint about it.

"Oh." Josie nodded a little too vigorously. What was she going to do? If word got out that Beatrice was so…unpleasant…it would be terrible for her and for the PR firm. But how was she going to hide it?

Quickly she realized what she had to do, the only thing she *could* do. She—Beatrice's publicist—had to keep Beatrice quiet and out of the public eye as much as possible.

No wonder everyone had bowed out so Josie could have this "plum" assignment. No one wanted it!

"Hot as hell in here," Beatrice said, fanning her face with her hand.

It was the perfect segue. "We've reserved a wonderful air-conditioned suite for you on the top floor," Josie told her. "Plenty of room for all of you. In fact, I think you'll enjoy it in there. There's a wide-screen TV, a fully stocked minibar and a refrigerator. You might not want to leave the room once you see it." She gave a light laugh while sending up a fervent prayer. "Oh, and we sent up some Rocky Top Beer, too, which you can take home with you."

It was like throwing a cocktail meatball to a hungry rottweiler. Beatrice looked satisfied for a moment, but then she frowned deeply and snarled, "I hope I don't have to take all them stairs to get up there." She looked dubiously at the gorgeous sweep of a stairway.

"No, no, there's an elevator in the hall," Josie assured her. The pleasant expression she had frozen on her face was beginning to melt. She couldn't keep this up much longer. She took Beatrice's key out of her pocket. "Here's your room key. I'll show you the way." She led Beatrice and her small entourage toward the elevator.

"So," she said as they walked, searching the air for something to say that wouldn't bring criticism. "I understand you're going to be cooking some of your famous dishes while you're here. How fun."

"Nothing fun about cooking," Beatrice said, sniffing.

"No?" Josie was surprised. She thought that, at least, was something Beatrice felt warmly about. "But people love your recipes. Surely you must enjoy creating them."

Beatrice snorted. "Nope. It's a *gift.*" She spat the word as if it were a gnat that had flown into her mouth. "Damn gift. All the women in my family have it. My grandmother, my mother. Sister missed the boat, though. Madge." Her mouth turned down at the corners into a very unpleasant expression when she said *Madge.* "She's jealous that I got it."

"She doesn't cook?"

Beatrice heaved her heavy shoulders. "Haven't seen her in more'n five years."

"Oh, that's too bad."

Beatrice nodded, and for a moment Josie thought she spotted a little tenderness. "Too bad it ain't been ten years," she said.

Josie nodded and pressed the up button for the elevator.

They waited.

"So. The Beaujold women have a gift for cooking," she said, pressing the button again. Where was the elevator? The inn only had five floors. How long did it take an elevator to get from top to bottom?

Beatrice stared at her with beady eyes. "Wickham women. And the gift is for bewitchin' men," she said with an absurd swing of her hips. "Seducing 'em. They cannot resist. The recipes," she finished, "are simply *how* we do it."

"Lots of people seem to think the recipes work magic," Josie said, thinking of Buffy and others she'd met who swore by the book. She'd never given the idea much credit, but she was surprised at the number of stories she had heard of men making proposals—proper and otherwise—over chilis and hot cakes from the book.

"You got a husband?" Beatrice asked unexpectedly.

"Not at the moment, no." She saw a change in Beatrice's expression and added quickly, before she could be accused of being a half-dressed lesbian, "Someday, maybe, but right now I'd rather not get tied down."

"Smart girl." Beatrice thumped a meaty finger against her temple. "That's where I made my mistake. Shoulda just played the field." She cocked her head toward her granddaughter. "Tried to tell Cher that, but she got it all confused and had a baby." She shook her head. "Girl's got nothin' upstairs. Nothin'."

Cher gave her aunt a look of sheer hatred.

"Remember to get them cheesecakes out of the car when you've unloaded your stuff, girl," Beatrice barked, then said to Josie, "They asked me to bring them cheesecakes of mine, even though they're gonna bring nothin' but trouble. Haven't met a man yet who didn't turn into a horn dog on eatin' them. 'Course, it's like that with most of my recipes, but the creamy ones in particular. Chocolate pudding, cheesecake. Guess people like to spread it on their body parts or something, I don't know."

"Excuse me," said a small voice from behind Josie.

Josie turned to see Lily Rose from the front desk. "The elevator is out of order."

"Out of order?" Josie repeated. "When will it be fixed?"

"Oh, we've called the handyman already," she said, as if that would mean something to Josie. "But since it's after hours now, he was already in bed. He's on the way, though." She looked at Beatrice. "In the meantime, Ms. Beaujold, can I show you to your room?"

"Well, *some*body better," Beatrice said, with a look that implied Josie had better fix the elevator herself if the handyman didn't come through.

Beatrice stopped and turned back. "You the one with my check?" she asked Josie.

"I'm sorry?" Josie asked, although she knew full well what Beatrice was getting at.

"The check. My appearance fee for comin' here. They said you'd have it ready for me." She held a meaty hand out. "Let's have it."

It took Josie a moment to formulate the words.

"I...I don't have it on me. It's in my briefcase." That much was true. "I'll get it to you later."

Beatrice frowned. "I don't work until I have it in my hand. Make no mistake."

It was an interesting choice of words, considering Josie had already made about fifty. "Don't worry about a thing," Josie said, as brightly as she could. "You just go on up and get some rest."

Beatrice wasn't so easily distracted. "You'll have the check for me then?"

"Absolutely." Somehow. Even if she had to write it herself. It probably wouldn't bounce until *after* Beatrice got home.

Apparently satisfied, Beatrice gave a nod and dragged Cher and Britney off behind Lily, just as Dan Duvall approached.

"I've been looking for you," he said.

Gooseflesh rose on her arms and she rubbed her hands across them. "Did you find my briefcase?"

"Not yet. But—"

He was interrupted by a small pack of women flouncing by. An impossibly buxom platinum blonde tossed a seductive look over her shoulder and said, "Hey, Dan. Long time. What's the matter, don't you like me anymore?"

"Now, what do you think, Kathy?" He gave a smile that had probably gotten *Kathy* to agree to any number of unholy things.

"I think it's been too long," she cooed. She didn't even glance at Josie. "I've been thinking about you a *lot*."

"Always nice to be appreciated," Dan drawled. He would have tipped his cap if he'd been wearing one.

Josie watched with disgust as the girl blew him a kiss and walked away, swinging her hips enough to shake a martini if she'd had a hip flask.

"You were saying, *Chief?*" Josie asked impatiently. Then she noticed he was holding a manilla envelope. "Hey, is that mine?"

He handed it to her. "That's what I was going to ask you."

She took it with eager hands and turned it over. There, in her handwriting, was the name Beatrice Beaujold. "Yes," she said, hurriedly opening it to see if her papers were inside. *Please,* she prayed silently, *please let them be there.* Maybe—just maybe—this weekend would turn out okay, after all.

Maybe no one would find out what Beatrice was really like.

Maybe Beatrice wouldn't find out her editor had told Josie what she was really like.

Maybe Josie would still have a job when she got back to New York.

Except that the envelope felt awfully thin. She loosened the brad and looked inside. Her neatly filed papers were gone. There were just a few dirty scraps inside. "What's this?" she asked, suddenly feeling like crying. No letter from Beatrice's editor and no check. She was still in huge trouble.

"I was hoping you'd know. The envelope was empty when we found it. There were just a few papers scattered around it. If there were more, they must have blown away.''

"Was there no sign of my briefcase? The rest of my things?"

"Only this." He reached into his pocket and pulled out a smashed piece of a shiny brass lock. "Look familiar?"

She took it. It was from her case. "Yes."

"That's what I thought." He reached for the envelope. "I'm particularly concerned about this." He took out several of the pieces of paper and started piecing them together.

"What the…" It was Beatrice's publicity photos, torn into long, even strips. Josie took them, then took a step backward and sat down on the end of a brocade-covered chaise longue. It squeaked under her weight, emphasizing the silence between herself and Dan. "It looks like there's some sort of writing on it," she said, assembling the pieces on her lap.

It wasn't writing, at least not all of it. Most of it was drawing, in thick black marker. Someone had adorned Beatrice's face with horns and a black beard, then put a big *X* over the whole thing. Across the top, the word *whore* was scrawled.

Now, truthfully, *bitch* Josie might have understood, but *whore?*

"Do you have any idea why someone might have done this?" Dan asked, looking at her with sharp eyes.

"None."

"No enemies?" He raised an eyebrow. "No one who might have something against her?"

Josie had only known Beatrice for a couple of hours, but it was easy to imagine why any number of people might draw horns on her picture. She thought again of the missing letter from Susan Pringle and wondered wildly what it might have said that was "confidential." What had, just a few hours ago, seemed a cursory caution now took on sinister overtones. Had Beatrice been arrested at some point? Did she have a secret life that no one could know about? Did that have something to do with what was happening now?

"I don't know of anyone in particular," Josie said slowly.

He cocked his head slightly and looked at her, his blue eyes as coercing as an interrogation lamp. It was a far cry from the languid indifference he'd shown earlier. "You sure?"

"I honestly don't know anything about her private life." She didn't add that she didn't *want* to know anything about Beatrice's private life.

"All right," Dan said after a moment. "You let me know if anything occurs to you, all right?" He reached into his pocket and took out his business card. "This has numbers for the station, my beeper and home."

Their fingertips brushed as she took the card. Josie looked at it, wondering how many women he'd given his card to. "Funny, you didn't give me one of these earlier. I thought you were too busy to bother with me.''

He leveled his gaze on her and gave a rakish smile. ''Were you looking to call me?''

''I mean, I thought you were too busy to bother with the matter of my stolen property.''

He shifted his weight and regarded her coolly. ''As I recall, you barely gave me a chance to say or do anything. But I'm saying it now—call if you need to.''

''And if I can find a phone.''

''There's one in the hall here,'' he said, as if that was plenty. ''Now, if you don't mind, I'd like to keep the papers as evidence. Just in case.''

''Go ahead. They're not going to do me much good.'' She held the envelope out to him.

''It's probably just a kid's prank,'' he said, taking it. ''It looks like it. But we'll keep an eye on it.''

Suddenly there was a long, loud howl from upstairs. Then there was an even louder thump, and a low rumble like thunder. Dan dashed into the lobby with Josie close behind, just as something enormous came tumbling down the stairs.

Beatrice!

Chapter Three

OYSTERS ROCKEFELLER
(from page 22 of *The Way to a Man's Heart*
by Beatrice Beaujold)

Mother always said, The fresher the oysters, the fresher the man you feed them to.

36 fresh oysters on the half shell
$^1/_2$ cup sour cream
1 teaspoon each salt and pepper
1 teaspoon finely minced garlic
6 tablespoons butter
$^1/_2$ cup finely minced raw watercress
3 tablespoons minced onion
2 tablespoons finely minced green onion
3 tablespoons minced parsley

*5 tablespoons fine bread crumbs mixed with 2 table-spoons Parmesan cheese
Tabasco sauce to taste
$^1/_2$ teaspoon Pernod (or other anise-flavored liqueur)
$^1/_2$ teaspoon table salt
$^1/_2$ lb. rock salt*

Remove oysters from shells and put 1 teaspoon of the sour cream, which has been mixed with the salt, pepper and garlic, into each shell. Place the oysters on top of the sour cream dollops. Refrigerate them while you prepare the sauce.

Melt the butter in a saucepan. Add the watercress, onion, green onion, parsley, bread-crumb mixture, Tabasco, liqueur and $^1/_2$ teaspoon salt. Cook, stir-ring constantly, for 15 minutes. Purée the mixture and let it cool.

Coat the bottom of a large oven-safe platter with rock salt. Set the oysters in the rock salt and divide the topping into 36 equal portions. Place one por-tion on each oyster. Broil until topping is brown. Serve.

For a moment, Josie stood rooted to the spot as Beatrice, seemingly in slow motion, thunked hard from step to step to landing to step to finally slump in a large heap on the floor. She looked like a huge pile of bedding.

Dan Duvall was the first to react. He was at Beatrice's side in three strides. He knelt on the floor, close but careful not to move her. Josie hurried over and stood by him while he pressed his fingers to her neck, then to her wrist.

"Can you feel her pulse?" Josie asked.

"Yes," he said, his face etched with concentration. "It's strong."

"Call 911," Dan ordered Lily Rose from across the room. His voice rang with authority.

Lily Rose ran to the front desk in rapid ministeps.

"I'll do it," Josie said sharply. She wasn't all that confident that Lily Rose could make the call. She started to move toward the desk when she saw Lily Rose pick up the phone and make the call.

Then Beatrice moaned.

Josie turned back to her, relieved.

Dan leaned down toward the older woman. "Ma'am? Can you hear me?"

"I…hear…"

"Ma'am?" Dan said to Beatrice. "Ms. Beaujold?"

She moaned again.

Josie heard a man's voice behind her whisper to someone, "Neck could be broken."

Someone else said, "…think she slipped on one of her own oysters Rockefeller…."

"…best night of my life, thanks to her oysters Rockefeller recipe…"

Dan said to Josie, "Maybe if you talked to her. A familiar voice might help." He motioned for her to join him closer to Beatrice.

Josie knew her voice wasn't any more familiar to Beatrice than Dan's was, and that, what's more, it probably wouldn't be particularly comforting to her.

Still, it was easier just to try than to explain all of that.

She moved too close to Dan for her own comfort and laid a hand gingerly on Beatrice's forearm. "Are you all right?" she asked, then, realizing how lame it sounded, she added, "Beatrice? It's Josie. Ross. From Page-turner Promotions."

One eye opened and, after searching for a moment, landed on Josie. "What?"

"You've had a fall," Josie said to her. "Down the stairs. We've called for help, just—" she patted Beatrice the way she might have patted a snarling dog "—stay put."

Beatrice rolled her eyes, and for a moment Josie thought it was in pain, but it was quickly evident that it was merely impatience. "Where do you think I'm gonna go?"

Josie swallowed a sharp suggestion.

"Do you have any idea what happened?" Dan asked Beatrice.

Beatrice groaned again, this time in a way that struck Josie as being a little too dramatic. "I saw…pushed me…" Beatrice closed her eyes and let out a long breath.

"Who pushed you?" Dan asked sharply.

"Oh, my God, is she all right?" Buffy came running over from the direction of the stairs.

"Were you with her?" Dan asked.

"Yes. That is, I was there a couple of minutes before she fell. I was on my way up to my room when I heard the commotion."

"So you didn't see what happened?"

"No." She shook her head, her eyes wide as she looked at Dan. "She was fine when I was talking to her."

"Did you see anyone else around?"

"No one."

The crowd around them grew larger. People murmured softly to one another about the poor old woman.

Josie was just beginning to feel bad for thinking Beatrice might be playing it up when Beatrice opened both eyes and looked around again, this time lowering her brow menacingly. "What the hell are you all staring at?"

The crowd went silent.

"Get out of here," Beatrice said, her voice growing stronger, although she waved her arm feebly. "Out!"

"Ms. Beaujold will not be making any public appearances tonight," Josie announced. "But you can see her in the display room tomorrow afternoon at two, when she signs copies of her book."

Although there were interested murmurs, no one left.

"Okay, everyone, back off," Dan said. "She's going to be fine."

A thin man in the front of the crowed asked, "Should we get her a glass of water?"

Beatrice managed to gather enough strength to spew one insult. "What the hell do you think water's going to do, you damn fool? Get me a beer."

The man turned pink. His eyes flitted to Josie, and he turned even pinker.

She searched frantically for a way to alleviate his embarrassment. "That was a good idea," she said, half-expecting one of Beatrice's tree trunk arms to swing out and knock her over. "But I think I hear the paramedics."

Beatrice struggled to her elbows. "I hope you didn't call them on my account." Her breathing was labored as she sat up. "If you did, send 'em home. I don't want any strange men poking and prodding at me."

Josie tried to imagine how the strange young men would feel about poking and prodding at Beatrice, but she remained silent.

"Take a picture!" Beatrice barked at a woman who stepped too close as she passed by. She passed her glare to another woman who was standing several feet away. "What are *you* looking at? And where'd you get that shirt?" Her voice was still weak, but she managed to muster the strength she needed to add, "Looks like a damn slipcover!"

Josie had to bite her tongue to keep from reprimanding Beatrice in front of everyone. She was offending people right and left. Hurting the feelings of fans who may have come a long way just to meet her. It was like watching a train wreck.

"Now…Beatrice," Josie said, in a voice far more gentle than she felt. "You're not quite being yourself. You must have hit your head."

She was almost glad when Beatrice leaned back

and said to Dan, "It's hard to breathe with all these *spectators* crowding round."

"Please give us some privacy," Josie commanded. "She's fine and she appreciates your concern, but she needs a little breathing room. But there's free beer on the porch, along with some of Beatrice Beaujold's famous vanilla cheesecake."

The crowd dispersed, murmuring appreciatively about free food and drink. Josie returned to Beatrice and Dan.

"Who pushed you?" he asked Beatrice quietly.

She paused, then said, "No. No one."

"But you just said…"

"I was mistaken. Must have been a mirror up there or something, made me think I saw another person."

"What were you doing up there?"

"As you know, the damn elevator is broken. I had to take the damn stairs." She gave Josie a contemptuous look.

The doors burst open and two eager-looking paramedics rushed in with a narrow stretcher. When they saw Beatrice lying on the floor they stopped and looked at each other, then at the stretcher.

"Get them outta here," Beatrice growled.

"Let them look you over, Beatrice," Josie said, bracing herself for yet another fight. It was quickly becoming clear to her why no one else had taken this assignment. It wasn't because they were giving a plum client to the new girl, it was because the new girl was perhaps the only one in the firm who didn't know how very difficult Beatrice was to deal with.

"No. Nothing's wrong with me."

Dan looked at Josie with raised eyebrows. "What do you think?" he asked under his breath.

"I don't know. Maybe we should ask her niece, Cher. At least she's family. She's up in the suite. I'll get her."

"No, I'll go," Dan volunteered. He looked at the paramedics. "Mike, Len, you mind waiting a few minutes, just to be sure you're not taking her with you?"

"No problem, Dan," the smaller one said, and Dan nodded and took off toward the stairs.

He was stopped before he got there by Jerry, who was holding a pen and notepad and asking, "Am I too late?"

"Too late for what?" Dan asked impatiently.

"To cover the story. I heard Ms. Beaujold had a fall so I ran out to get my paper from the car."

"What the hell do you mean *cover the story?*"

"Oh, didn't I tell you?" Jerry looked smug. "I got a job. I'm writing for the *Beldon Chronicle.*"

"Since when?"

"Since I offered them my services." Jerry smiled. "They *leapt* at the chance to have me, unlike certain other people I know."

Dan opened his mouth to ask for an explanation. "I don't have time for this," he said, brushing past Jerry. "You can tell me about it later. But for now, yes, you're too late. There's no story here." He stopped and looked very seriously at Jerry. "I *mean* it. Don't go trying to make this into something."

"I'm just looking for a good scoop, bro'."

"Yeah? Well, this ain't it." With one final stern look, he turned and went up the stairs to find Beatrice Beaujold's niece.

It was hard to believe the vandalized photo was a prank, Dan thought as he took the stairs by twos. He'd thought so from the beginning. For one thing, kids didn't usually target elderly women, and for another, the word *whore* didn't make sense for a random joke on an old woman's picture. But now that she may have been pushed down the stairs, it was *really* hard to believe it was all a joke.

When he got to the first landing, where Beatrice had fallen from, he noticed there was no mirror. There also wasn't anything that could be mistaken for another person. Unless, of course, it *had* been another person.

When he got to the door to Beatrice's suite, he had to knock several times before Cher answered the door. He could hear the *Jerry Springer* show blasting from the television in the other room.

"Yeah?"

"Are you Cher?" he asked.

"Yeah."

He automatically put on his "notifying family" voice. "Everything seems to be all right, but your aunt has had an accident."

She looked at him and blinked, utterly emotionless.

"She fell down the stairs," he said, in response to

the question she should have asked but didn't. He watched for a reaction, but there was none.

He cleared his throat. "And, as I said, she appears to be all right, but the paramedics are downstairs and they're ready to take her in for a checkup, but she insists that she doesn't want to go. Ms. Ross thought we should consult with you before letting them go."

Cher straightened herself. "So let her stay. She'll just do whatever she wants, anyway." A baby's cry came from the other room and she sighed. "I gotta go."

Before Dan could respond, she shut the door.

He'd done everything he could, he decided on his way back down. It wasn't like he could *force* the old woman to go to the ER, even though it's what he would have done if it was his own aunt who'd been hurt.

When he got back, Josie and Beatrice were sitting on a sofa in the lobby. Josie's shirt was wet and there was a half-empty glass of water on the table next to her.

"She didn't *want* any water," Josie said through her teeth, in answer to his unspoken question. "Just like she already said once, dammit."

Dan tried not to smile. The old woman was a bit abrasive. If he was looking for people who didn't like her, it might not be hard to find at least a handful of suspects.

His smile faded instantly, though, when he saw Buzz Dewey making his way through the crowd, huffing over toward them.

"What's going on?" Buzz asked fretfully. "Has someone been hurt?"

"It was just a little accident. Ms. Beaujold fell down the stairs, but I think she's gonna be just fine."

"Ms. Beaujold!" Buzz exclaimed, his face going even more pale than usual. "Oh, no!"

"She's just fine, Buzz. Honestly. I think she's a little, er, stronger than you imagine."

Buzz turned his attention to Beatrice. "Ms. Beaujold," he said in a tremulous voice. "I'm Buzz Dewey, the president of Rocky Top Beer, and I hope you'll accept my sincerest apologies for what's happened. Is there anything I can do to make you more comfortable?"

The older woman appeared to consider the question for a moment before saying, "I could use a beer. Or two. A girl needs a nightcap."

Buzz looked surprised but tried to hide it, the effect being an expression of utter alarm.

The guys loved playing poker with Buzz Dewey.

"I'll get one, or two, for you immediately, of course." He hurried past Dan, looking straight ahead, as if he was on the most important mission of his life.

Dan turned his attention back to Beatrice Beaujold. He was going to have to keep a close eye on her. Buzz may have been more right than he realized to worry about her.

"I *told* you if I *wanted* water, I'd *ask* for water," Beatrice said testily to Josie. "Lord, girl, don't you understand English? Let me be, now."

"Beatrice," Josie said, taking a short breath in

through her nose. "It's my *job* to look after you. Just like it's *your* job to meet and greet your public with a *smile*." She hissed the last word through her teeth and Dan had to try not to laugh.

"Not till I've been paid," Beatrice muttered.

"Ms. Ross," Dan interrupted, "may I have a word with you?"

Josie hesitated, then, with a glance in Beatrice's direction, nodded. "All right." She got up and picked her way over to him, her shapely legs a sharp contrast to the thick, inert ones Ms. Beaujold refused to move to make Josie's passage easier.

"I'll get right to the point," Dan said when they were alone. "I think your friend there *may* be in danger."

"Yeah," she scoffed. "From me."

"Ms. Ross, I'm serious."

Her annoyed expression changed to one of serious attention. "Really?"

"Well, now, I don't know anything for sure. But the evidence does suggest that there's someone out there who doesn't like her."

"What kind of danger are you thinking she's in? You think someone's going to vandalize her picture again or something worse?"

He didn't want to alarm her, but his instincts said there was more to this than met the eye. "No idea. Most cases, it turns out to be nothing. Just the same, I'm going to be keeping an eye on her." He was more concerned about poor Buzz, who didn't need any more stress. From the look of her, Beatrice Beaujold could probably fend off an army by herself.

"Well, thanks," Josie said. "Just bear in mind that you'll need to stay out of the way while Beatrice interacts with her public."

Dan snorted. "Her *public?*"

"Yes," Josie said shortly. "The people who are coming from all over the country to meet her. Her cookbook is very popular, you know."

He'd seen it. It was hard to believe that many people were going to be flocking to see Beatrice Beaujold and learn her supposed man-luring secrets.

"Yes," Josie said. There was a definite "Wanna make something of it?" tone to her voice, but before she could actually say it, there was a whoop from Beatrice's direction and she held an overflowing beer bottle in the air before throwing it back and consuming what appeared to be half the bottle.

"*She's* giving advice on how to lure men," Dan confirmed, holding back a smile.

Josie glared at him. "Look, just do your job and I'll do mine, all right?"

"Funny you should say that, since you and your friend Beatrice are the very things standing in the way of me doing just that."

She stepped back and put her hand on her hip. "Just how do you figure that?"

"I'm already down three men on my force. The men and women who are still here are so overworked that a handful of them are ready to quit. Add this damn chili cook-off to that, along with all the problems that *always* come with it, and you'd think things couldn't get worse.'' His blue eyes went steely. ''Unless someone brings some pain-in-the-butt cookbook author and her hoity-toity publicist into the mix and wants them to have extra protection.''

''I don't need your protection,'' Josie objected hotly. ''I'm more than capable of taking care of myself.''

''Big talk from a woman who's already been at the center of two police reports today.''

''Neither of which was my fault.''

''Debatable.''

She narrowed her eyes. ''I'm afraid I don't have time for a debate right now, Chief Duvall. I have business to conduct. And at the moment *you* are standing in the way of *that.*''

Without waiting for an answer, she pushed past him and kept walking until she was certain she was out of his sight.

Chapter Four

VANILLA CHEESECAKE
(from page 91 of *The Way to a Man's Heart*
by Beatrice Beaujold)

Vanilla is one of the most potent man-luring ingredients there is. Use the best you can find and this
creamy dessert will fortify you for a long and plea-
surable night ahead.

*32 oz. cream cheese (4 8-oz. packages), room tem-
perature so it whips lighter*
1 2/3 cups superfine sugar
1/4 cup cornstarch
1 tablespoon vanilla extract
seeds from 1 vanilla bean

*4 drops fiori di sicilia (or use lemon extract if you
can't get fiori di sicilia)*
1 pinch salt
¹/₂ teaspoon ground nutmeg
³/₄ cup whipping cream
2 eggs
2 ready-made graham cracker piecrusts, deep dish

Place one 8-oz. package of the cream cheese, ¹/₃
cup of the sugar and the cornstarch in a mixing
bowl and whip together for 2 minutes before adding
the rest of the cream cheese.

Next add the remaining sugar, vanilla, vanilla bean
seeds, *fiori di sicilia,* salt, nutmeg and whipping
cream and put the mixer on high for 3 minutes.

Add the eggs and beat for 20 seconds more, then
stop the mixer.

Pour the cheese filling into the ready-made piecrusts
and set them on a jelly roll sheet with ¹/₄ inch of
water.

Bake 60 minutes or until the center of the cheesecake is firm.

Cover with foil and cool overnight in the refrigerator. Serve chilled.

Josie got to Beatrice just as she was forcing her
unstable form upright.

"I think I'll just go upstairs and get a little shut-
eye," Beatrice slurred. "It's been a hell of a long
day."

"A fine idea," Buzz Dewey said. "And I'm happy

to report that the elevator is fully operational again, per your request.''

''Good, good, you are a fine man.'' She smiled thinly. ''Perhaps you'd like to try some of my cheesecake….''

Josie stepped between them. ''I'll see you to your room, Beatrice,'' she said, with a dismissive nod to Buzz Dewey. ''I'd like to have a word with you about the book.''

Beatrice looked impatient. ''But Mr. Dewey was just going to have a bite of my cheesecake.''

''I'm most eager to try it,'' Buzz said, with the hopeful look of a child in front of a candy shop.

''Great,'' Josie said briskly. Then to Beatrice, she added, ''I'll just need a few minutes of your time now and then you can go up and get to sleep.''

''Fine, fine.'' Beatrice leaned heavily on her cane. ''You are a pushy one.''

Josie resisted the urge to point out the irony of Beatrice's accusation.

They hadn't moved ten feet before Beatrice stopped and said, ''I want a beer for the road.''

''Fine.'' Josie gritted her teeth. ''You wait here. I'll get it.''

She returned to where Buzz Dewey was still sitting, looking fretfully in Beatrice's direction. This, Josie realized, was just the opportunity she needed.

''Mr. Dewey,'' Josie said in a quiet voice as she approached. ''I'm afraid we have a small problem.''

She might have told him his hair was on fire for the look he gave her. ''We do?''

"Just a small one," she said in her most soothing voice. "You see, the check you sent for Beatrice's appearance was stolen and we need a replacement."

"Stolen? My goodness."

"I don't think it's cause for great concern," she continued. "No one else can cash it. But the problem is, Beatrice is used to being paid in advance for this kind of thing and—" she shrugged broadly "—I'm sure you see the problem."

"Indeed I do." He nodded. "The banks are closed tomorrow so we cannot do anything to stop payment on that stolen check until Monday."

Josie hesitated. Was he saying he wasn't going to give Beatrice another one? "That's unfortunate, but in the meantime we really need to get Beatrice a replacement check. Just to show good faith, you understand."

He clicked his tongue against his teeth. "It's out of the question, I'm afraid. But on Monday morning I'll have one ready bright and early."

Josie counted to five, then said, "Mr. Dewey, I'm sure your intentions are good, but Beatrice..." She searched for a good reason to insist on getting another check. "Beatrice has been burned by this kind of mistake before. I'm afraid she's going to be reluctant to fulfill her duties until you've fulfilled yours."

"But we did. We sent the check weeks ago."

It was true. Hard to argue with. "Could you just try? Please?"

"Well..."

"Please, Mr. Dewey." She placed a hand gently on his forearm. "Just try."

He blushed to the roots of his hair. "I'll do it."

"Thank you so much." Josie smiled, but her relief was short-lived.

She still had to tell Beatrice about the police chief's theory on her safety.

"Where's the beer?" Beatrice demanded when Josie returned.

Josie swallowed a harsh oath, then said, "It's chilling in the refrigerator in your room."

"Better be."

"Beatrice, we need to talk about something."

"You lost the check."

"What? No, I didn't lose the check. Of course not." Her forced laugh would have been an obvious sign of guilt in any kindergarten classroom. "No, no, I'm afraid it's much more serious than that." She suspected that nothing could be more serious than that for Beatrice.

When they reached a quiet hallway, Josie carefully explained to Beatrice about the picture and bio and the concerns that Dan Duvall had for her safety. When she was finished, instead of expressing a little gratitude that people were looking out for her, Beatrice just gave Josie a hard glare.

"So?"

Josie was confused. "So…what?"

"Exactly. So what?" Beatrice gave a snort that was unmistakably derisive. "Girl, I've looked down the barrel of a twelve-gauge without spilling a drop of pee...."

Josie winced.

"...I'm sure as hell not going to cower just because some fool drew a beard on my picture."

"But, Beatrice, it's not just that. When you first came to after falling down the stairs you said you'd been pushed. The police are concerned that someone may be out to harm you."

"To hell with the cops!" Beatrice boomed. "I don't want them within twenty yards of me."

Reflexively, Josie raised a finger to her lips. "Please. Let's not create a scene." It was difficult to comprehend Beatrice's hostility. Didn't she care that someone may be trying to hurt her? Wasn't she even a little grateful that people were trying to *help* her? "The police are concerned for your safety."

"I don't want any damn cops hanging around me," Beatrice snapped. "It's the cops that ruined my girl-hood."

Josie felt as if she was standing before a pool of muck, without any way past except stepping right through it.

Beatrice stared at her, obviously waiting for her to ask for an explanation.

"The police here seem very nice," Josie hedged, thinking that Dan Duvall wasn't nice so much as he *looked* nice. Big difference.

"Police ruined my girlhood," Beatrice repeated. "Arrested my daddy for making his special tonic in the backyard." She shook her head ruefully, showing the first real—albeit small—sign of emotion Josie had seen from her. "Eventually they arrested Mama, too. Prostitution, my behind."

Josie's eyes widened. "Pros—"

"So you keep the police clear of me. If they don't bother me, I won't bother them."

That, at least, was good news. "You won't? You promise?"

Beatrice scowled. "Are we finished?"

"Yes." Josie pressed the elevator button for her. Mercifully the doors opened right up. "Enjoy your rest." She needed some rest herself. Like three days of it. Then maybe—just *maybe*—she would feel up to dealing with all of this.

"I always do," Beatrice said, stepping onto the elevator. "Especially on the rare occasion I'm able to do it alone."

It didn't bear thinking about.

So Josie tried, all the way back to the lobby, *not* to think about it.

"You tell her about the threats?" Dan asked when she came back in. He was holding a paper plate with a piece of cheesecake on it.

Josie remembered Beatrice's theory about why people liked the cheesecake and pudding, and fought a mental image of Buzz Dewey covered in it.

"Hard at work, Chief Duvall?" she asked, picturing, instead, Dan covered in it. It was good. This was bad. The stress must really be getting to her.

"As always," he said, in the same voice he may have used to say that, yes, he would have another mint julep after a dip in the pool. He looked at her for a moment, then gestured with his fork and plate. "You should try this. It's really good."

"Actually, I have work to do," she said in a clipped voice.

"Don't we all."

"I'm not stopping you from doing your job."

"No?"

"No. I'm just trying to do mine. And if that's inconvenient for you for some reason, I'm sorry."

He gave a short laugh. "If that's inconvenient for me, you're not sorry at all. You'd just bulldoze right on over anyone who got in your way. See, that's the problem with you."

"Excuse me?" Indignance welled in her. "The *problem* with me?"

"Mmm." He nodded. "You come from this dog-eat-dog world and you can't turn it off."

"Chief Duvall, you don't know anything about me."

He gave a laconic shrug. "You may be surprised at what I know about you."

"Really." She raised her chin so she could look down her nose at him. "Do tell."

He sized her up for a moment before speaking. "You live in an apartment alone, probably. No roommate. You don't like having other peoples' stuff lying around your place. You want everything in order."

He was exactly right. She'd only lived with a roommate once, and she'd moved out after just a month because she could never find her things when she needed them.

"A lot of people live alone," she said, though some of the force had left her voice. "It's hardly surprising that you could guess that."

"Wait a minute, now, I'm not finished." He regarded her as an artist choosing the best composition, then said, "You're meticulous about your diet. Maybe a vegetarian."

He was wrong. She did eat chicken and fish occasionally.

"A little meat now and then wouldn't kill you," he continued, in a tone that made her wonder if they were really talking about diet at all. "You ought to give it a try."

"Nothing you've said so far impresses me," she said. "You haven't said anything that a carnival gypsy couldn't come up with."

"You're not saying I'm wrong."

"It's hard to be wrong when you're being so general."

"Okay, you want me to get more specific? You're a night person but you get up early in the morning. You don't get enough sleep. That's not good for you."

"Thanks, Doctor." The accuracy of his assessment was making her uncomfortable.

"Of course," he lowered his voice, "that could all be solved by a little physical exertion before bed. But you don't do that, either. Least not lately."

Her jaw dropped. "I beg your pardon!"

"Now, don't get huffy, it's nothing to be ashamed of. Intimacy is a basic human need. We all go a little crazy without it."

"Not that it's any of your business, but I get all the *exertion* I need."

He shook his head. "If you did, you'd sleep better. You'd be a little more relaxed."

"I cannot believe you're saying this to me."

"You asked for it."

She gave a derisive snort. "Yeah, well, you're no psychic. Stick to your day job. Although I can't say you're brilliant at that, either."

He was unperturbed. "I'm just saying you'd be a lot happier if you loosened up a little. Live a little instead of trying to micro-manage everything. Have a beer once in a while. Eat something that isn't good for you. Do something just because it feels good. Do it twice if it feels real good."

Her breath felt shallow in her chest. "I do plenty of that. *All* of that."

He gave a knowing smile that infuriated her. "Prove it."

"How?"

"Here." He moved closer to her.

She looked up at him, her breath trapped in her throat, along with her heart. He was going to kiss her, she knew it, and she wanted him to. It was crazy, it was wrong, but she wanted it. "Yes?" she breathed.

He cut off a piece of cheesecake and held the fork out to her. "Try a bite."

Her heart dropped back into her stomach and her breath left in one long hiss. "No, thanks."

"What did you think I was going to say?" he asked, setting the plate down.

"I didn't think you were going to say anything."

He smiled, clearly aware of what she was thinking and amused by it. "So what did you think I was going to do?"

Her face went hot. "Nothing. Here, I'll try the cheesecake if it will shut you up." She took a bite, and it was, indeed, delicious.

Dan, however, was still looking at her in a way that suggested their business wasn't finished. He lifted her chin with two fingers. "Did you think I was going to kiss you?"

"Of course not," she said, but she knew her scarlet face gave her away.

"Is that what you want?"

Yes! her body screamed, ignoring her mind's objection. Fortunately, her mouth was working for her mind. "What I *want,* Chief, is for you to find my things."

He didn't remove his hand. "That's an interesting way of putting it."

"I—I didn't mean..." she stammered, but she didn't get to finish her sentence before he lowered his mouth onto hers.

Her anger dissolved like smoke in the wind, leaving behind a storm of desire. She sank against him, relishing the feel of his body against hers.

His arms encircled her, making her feel both safe

and in danger at the same time. It was a delicious combination that left her knees weak and her heart pounding.

This was foolish, a voice in her head warned. This guy was a playboy with no real respect for women. There was no way a real relationship would come out of this, so she was just setting herself up for disappointment. For waiting for calls that wouldn't come, and hoping for a repeat performance she'd never get to see.

Yet, at the moment, one performance seemed sufficient. So deep was her hunger for him that she would, at that moment, have gone against every one of her principles for just one more taste of him.

He drew back, smiling. "That better?"

Her knees did fail her and she tottered slightly. "Absolutely not," she said weakly.

He laughed softly. "Then I apologize for being so forward. See, I've been wanting to do that since I first saw you."

Her heart was still pounding so hard she thought she might pass out, but she didn't want him to know that. "Well, now you have." She raised her eyebrows at him. "Satisfied?"

"Sweetheart, it takes a lot more than that to satisfy me," he said, his voice quiet. "How about you?"

She swallowed. She didn't know if it was the lack of sleep, some kind of rebound thing, or magic in the cheesecake, but for reasons she couldn't understand, Dan Duvall was pounding through her defenses. "I'm going up to bed. I mean to sleep. Alone," she added unnecessarily.

There was laughter in his eyes. "Glad you cleared that up. You have a little bit of cream…" He raised his hand to her cheek and wiped the corner of her mouth with his thumb.

She didn't draw back, although she knew she should.

"You're very pretty, you know that?" He left his hand there, his thumb slowly caressing her cheek.

"And you're very smooth."

He laughed. "And you're very suspicious."

"Shouldn't I be?"

"I don't know. Depends on what you suspect."

She removed his hand and took a step back. "I suspect you're trying to add another notch to your belt."

"The thought never occurred to me," he said slowly. "Although I'd be glad to put a notch in yours, if you like. Weren't you saying something about going to your room…?"

"Thanks, but I'm not sure where your notch has been. Besides, my belt is in my suitcase and, as you may recall, that's gone. In fact, I think your time would be much better spent trying to solve crimes, *Chief.*" It took some doing, but Josie turned on her heel and went to the elevator without looking back.

Still, she could feel his eyes on her.

After waiting for what seemed an eternity, and pushing the button about fifteen or twenty times, she was joined by Buffy Singer.

"Hey," Buffy said. "Are you okay? You look like you've seen a ghost."

"No, I just—I'm fine." She was anything but fine. In truth, she felt completely rattled. "How about you? Did you meet Beatrice earlier?"

"Yes, I did." A moment passed. "She's not quite how I pictured her."

This was exactly what Josie was afraid of. "Sometimes magic happens in the most unlikely places."

"Her recipes are magic, that's for sure."

The elevator arrived and they both stepped onto it together.

"What's your favorite?" Josie asked, trying to divert her thoughts from Dan Duvall. That kiss. And what he'd said. And what he'd meant.

What *had* he meant?

Were his comments really suggestive, or was she reading too much into them?

She forced her mind back to the conversation with Buffy. "I guess that would have to be the sweet potato pudding, huh?"

Buffy nodded. "Although I'm partial to the slow-cooked pork chops myself. That's something even my Frank could prepare for me." She laughed. "Who knows? He might find they work a little magic for him, too."

The elevator stopped and the doors opened.

"You'll have to keep me posted," Josie said.

"Will do." Buffy gave a little wave as the doors closed again and the elevator moved up to Josie's floor.

She left the elevator and headed for her room, aware of a sense of loneliness she hadn't recognized before. Usually, she was so busy that she didn't have time to stop and think. So she'd successfully avoided contemplating relationships and the lack of relationships in her life. And sex. Dan was right, dammit, sex—no, *intimacy*—was distinctly lacking in her life.

She hated to think that sad fact was written all over her face.

And that Dan had not only seen it, but tasted it in her kiss.

Chapter Five

KENTUCKY BEER CHEESE
(from page 18 of *The Way to a Man's Heart*
by Beatrice Beaujold)

This dish will spice up your life and increase your circulation. Serve it as an appetizer and you might find yourself too busy for dinner.

$^1/_2$ lb. sharp cheddar cheese, grated
2 cloves garlic, minced
$^1/_2$ cup beer
1 pinch salt
1 pinch cayenne pepper
$^1/_2$ teaspoon Worcestershire sauce
couple of dashes Tabasco sauce

Combine everything in a food processor and process on till smooth.

Chill and spread on crackers or toast.

Dan was still thinking about Josie Ross the next morning. In a nutshell, Josie Ross was little more than an uptight city girl. She was haughty, impatient, quick-tempered, and she was so hell-bent on her work and her image that she didn't seem to have any awareness of, or appreciation for, the good things in life. It had gone against everything inside of her to take that bite of cheesecake. But she'd done it to spite him.

He knew from bitter experience to avoid her type.

So why did he keep thinking about her?

Why did his blood course through his veins like a Thoroughbred on a racetrack every time he caught even a glimpse of her? Why did his fingers ache to touch her and tousle that oh-so-perfect hair whenever he got within six feet of her? Why did his mind keep creeping back to thoughts of her that could never be repeated aloud in church?

It had to stop.

He was glad to see a diversion in the form of Lenora Whiting making her unsteady way toward him from the lobby of the inn. Lenora had lived in town for as long as Dan could remember. As a matter of fact, she'd looked eighty for as long as Dan could remember.

"Afternoon, Danny," she said with a tip of her head. "I'm glad to see you. I want to sell my crocheted beer-can hats this week during the cook-off."

Her eyes held that familiar capitalist gleam Dan saw so often in Beldon residents this time of year. "Do I need to get a special permit for that?"

"Yes, you do, Lenora. Just like last year." And the year before, and the year before. He hoped this time she would give up the idea and spare herself the embarrassment of building her hopes only to sell one beer-can hat.

He also hoped he wouldn't have to buy that one hat. He already had enough to outfit a small, delinquent troop of Boy Scouts.

"Oh, that's right," she said, tapping her chin, as if she'd just remembered. He could see in her eyes she was going to sell her hats, anyway, permit or no.

That's what people did around here this time of year.

"Even if I use the special sales rack I got for my bicycle?"

Oh, no, not the bicycle sales rack again. Every time Dan saw her peddling around with that hundred pound albatross, he thought of the little engine that could and the fact that some little engines *couldn't*. He didn't want to see Lenora get hurt.

"I think you might need a special permit just for that bicycle, Lenora," he said, hoping to dissuade her. He saw, out of the corner of his eye, her "sales bike" out the window, gleaming in the morning sunshine.

"Hmm. I'll go to city hall and inquire," she said. If she'd been Pinocchio, her nose would have poked Dan right in the chest.

"You do that, Lenora," he said, with a sigh. Despite his pleasant conversation with Lenora, he couldn't wait until the weekend was over. Come

Monday, he was going to get himself a case or two of Buzz's best, and he was going to kick back with his feet up and just breathe the air.

"Well, if you'll excuse me, Danny, I think I'd better go get started on that right now. Thank you, dearie. You're such a good boy." She reached up and patted his cheek with her cool, dry, powder-scented hand. "Your daddy'd be proud, God rest his soul."

"Thanks, Lenora," he said, watching with affection as she made her way back to the lobby. But despite his pleasant conversation with Lenora, he couldn't wait until the weekend was over. Come Monday, he was going to get himself a case or two of Buzz's best, and he was going to kick back with his feet up and just breathe the air.

"What next?" Dan muttered under his breath.

"Try some beer cheese, Danny?" Kathy Bailey approached him, holding out a plate with some crackers spread with the cheese mixture.

"No, thanks, Kath."

She pouted her lipstick-reddened lips. "Aw, come on, Danny. I made it myself. Just for you."

He sighed and took a cracker from the plate. "That's awfully nice of you, Kath, but you didn't have to bother." He put it in his mouth. It was really good. Sharp cheddar cheese with an extra kick.

Kathy stood back and eyed him. "What do you think?" She straightened her back, which had the effect of poking her chest out. He wasn't sure whether he was supposed to be assessing her chest or the cracker. "Good," he said, figuring he was safe either way.

"Wanna go out tonight? Or come to my place?"

He ate another cheese cracker. "Sorry, can't," he said with his mouth full. He swallowed. "Gotta work."

"You don't have to work *all* night, do you?" she asked, stepping toward him and laying a red-taloned hand on his chest.

It occurred to him that he preferred Josie's short, plain nails.

"Actually, I do, Kathy. I'm working twenty-four hours until this thing's over."

She looked frustrated. "Maybe you should have another cracker."

He took one, waved it at her in thanks and said, "I'd better go now." He left with her behind him, muttering something about "stupid recipes that don't work."

He was halfway across the lobby when he heard a loud grinding groan of metal and the electricity dipped for a moment.

"What the hell was that?" someone exclaimed, voicing Dan's thoughts perfectly.

"It came from outside!"

A group of people rushed to the back doors. Dan pushed his way through to the front of the crowd. The moment he stepped outside, the humidity hit him in the face like a hot, wet washcloth.

"It's the air conditioner," old Cauley Bright said as Dan approached. He gestured toward a long metal rod jammed into the huge outdoor compressor. "You reckon that fell out of an airplane?" He glanced upward and hunched his shoulders, bracing himself for another falling object.

Dan looked into the wide, earnest eyes of the older man and shook his head. "No, Cauley, it didn't fall out of the sky. In fact—" he looked at the rod more closely "—this is part of the rack from a car."

Cauley looked befuddled. "Whose?"

"I don't know," Dan said, trying to pull the rod out of the compressor. "But I've got a bad feeling it's mine."

"Chief?" A young boy came running over to Dan, his face flushed and excited.

"What's up, Tommy?" Dan asked.

"Your car." The boy's eyes were wide. "Someone did something to it."

He knew it. "The rack?" he asked, already sure of the answer.

"Yup. And the whirly light on top's been pulled clean off."

Dan sighed. This was the kind of thing that always happened during the cook-off, but this year, of all years, he *really* didn't have time for such shenanigans. The rack he could do without for now, but the light was another story. "You see who did it?"

The boy shrugged. "Some old woman."

Okay, so clearly Tommy wasn't going to be any help in solving this. Not that it mattered. Drunks, rowdy teenagers, there were a whole bunch of troublemakers at the cook-off.

What mattered now was that someone had to go over to Bob Watson's place and get another one, pronto. Fortunately, Bob—who supplied parts for all the cars on the force—stocked extras of everything.

"Anyone seen Hunter?" Dan asked a group of locals who were standing by. Steve Hunter was the newest member of the force, which meant he got the honor of running errands like this. "I need him to take my car over to Bob's place."

"Hunter left about fifteen minutes ago," Cauley said, giving a broad wink. "With, uh, one of the female contestants."

He'd almost certainly live to regret that, Dan thought, but said nothing.

"Want me to take your car on over to Bob's?" Jerry offered, coming upon the scene with the scrawny dark-haired girl who was Beatrice Beaujold's niece, and her baby. "I've got a little time between assignments."

Dan shook his head. "You know it's against policy."

"Dan*ny,* I've worked on the force." He widened his eyes and tipped his head ever so slightly in the direction of the girl, silently imploring Dan to go along with his story.

"I'll take it myself," Dan said, half tempted to embarrass Jerry by telling the truth. Maybe it would shut him up once and for all. But Dan doubted it. And besides, he just didn't have the heart to do that. "Thanks, anyway," he added gruffly.

Jerry beamed. "Sure. Anytime." He turned to the girl. "Working on the force gave me the hands-on experience I needed to be a good crime reporter...."

Dan went to his car in the back lot of the Silver Moon Inn. He didn't need this. He did not need this. He'd already given in to the fact that he was going to have to work practically around the clock this week, but between this and looking after Buzz's cookbook author—

who seemed to have troubles of her own—Dan was not at all sure there was enough time in the day for him to do everything he had to do.

When he got to the car, he was glad to see that the damage wasn't as bad as he'd feared. If Bob wasn't too backed up, he could probably put a new light on pretty quickly.

"Be about an hour and a half," Bob told him fifteen minutes later, looking over the damage. "Give or take. Whoever did this wasn't really trying to be careful."

"I can see that." Dan looked at his watch. "So you think about one-thirty?"

Bob gave a nod. "Sounds about right."

"All right," Dan said, resigned. He'd walk back to the station and take complaint calls until the car was ready. Lord knew there would be plenty of them.

He just wished he had more of those little cheese and cracker thingies Kathy had made.

Josie slept like the dead, despite the fact that she'd had nothing to wear except the terry-cloth robe she'd found in the closet. For years she'd been a nervous sleeper, waking at every tiny noise, so it was quite a surprise to her when she woke up to find it was already nearly eleven in the morning. Beatrice's book signing and meet-and-greet with fans was at two o'clock, which gave Josie plenty of time to go out and find some new clothes.

She brushed her hair, wiped the mascara smudges from under her eyes and went into the hall. It was sweltering. She went to use the hall bathroom, but it was occupied, so she took the stairs down. In the lobby it was only a little cooler, and lots of glistening people were waving paper fans in front of their faces and complaining about the heat.

"Air-conditioning's out," someone explained to Josie. "They're trying to fix it now."

"It must be ninety degrees in here," Josie commented.

"Ninety-six," another person said, gesturing toward an indoor thermometer.

What next? As if Beatrice's public appearances weren't going to be challenging enough, now they had to add suffocating heat to the mix.

Josie located a rest room, freshened up as best she could with no soap, shampoo, water or clean clothes, then went to the lobby to find out where she should shop.

She stopped at the front desk and asked, first, if anyone had turned in her suitcase. Not surprisingly, they hadn't. She then asked where she might find a clothing boutique to replace her stolen clothes. Lily Rose suggested a place called His Track, Her Rack opposite the Mulberry Street entrance to the police station.

Josie hesitated, wondering whether Lily Rose had misunderstood her question or if she'd misunderstood the answer.

"Clothes," she repeated, gesturing at her body for clarification. "I need a new outfit."

Lily Rose nodded. "They have real nice things there."

Josie frowned. "And it's called what?"

"His Track, Her Rack."

It sounded like a strip club. A badly named strip club.

"You're sure they have women's clothes?"

"Mmm-hmm. And auto parts."

"Auto parts," Josie repeated, and the girl nodded. So Josie thanked her and left, figuring there was a fair chance in this crazy town that the place existed, and if it didn't, it would probably be faster to look around town herself than wait for Lily Rose to think of another place.

The inn had become so stiflingly hot that the air outside seemed cool, although she could tell it was going to be a hot day. As Josie traversed the sidewalks along the same route she'd taken to the police station earlier, she couldn't help but slow her pace and admire the gingerbread town and colorful storefronts.

One in particular—the Beldon Cake Bakery—stopped her completely. In the window, there were at least ten gorgeously ornate cakes. Some were traditional wedding cakes with intricate icing lace and bows, and some were formed into shapes. There were children's cakes—a lamb and a drum—and one with a perfect icing rendition of Elvis's face. But in the center, there was an elaborate cake built in the exact shape of the Taj Mahal. Every detail was there, from the domed kiosks and gilded gates, right down to the colorful floral arabesques inlaid on the white marble arches.

Josie had to laugh. Of all the things she might have expected to see in the windows of Beldon shops, the Taj Mahal was nowhere on the list.

The jingle of keys sounded behind her, and Josie turned abruptly to find a petite woman with short red hair turning the lock on the door.

"Hey," she said with a warm smile. "Looking to buy a cake?"

"No, no, I was just passing by and the Taj Mahal caught my eye."

The woman laughed. "Most people around here thought it was a sand castle."

"Heck of a sand castle," Josie said, then extended her arm. "I'm Josie Ross, by the way."

"Fiona Breen." The woman shook her hand. Her green eyes were bright and smiling. "I own this shop."

"It's adorable." Josie looked in the window again, noticing, this time, the lettering on the glass that read Fiona Breen, Proprietor. "Actually, it's more than adorable. It's really unique."

Fiona clucked her tongue against her teeth. "I just wish I had more business. Some months I worry that I'll have to chuck it all and go back to a desk job." She shrugged one shoulder. "I'm not very good at self-promotion."

"Funny you should mention that, since it's exactly what I do. Maybe I could help you out a little, give you some pointers."

"That would be great." Fiona looked amazed. "What on earth brings you to Beldon? Are you promoting the cook-off or something?"

"No, not exactly. One of the authors my firm represents is here. Beatrice Beaujold."

"Ooh, her." Fiona grimaced. "I've heard about

her.'' She widened her eyes in sympathy. ''Wow, that must be a tough job.''

Josie felt a little like she'd been punched in the stomach. ''What do you mean?''

''You know, her little, um, *problem.*''

''Problem?''

Fiona looked embarrassed. ''My gosh, I'm so sorry. I thought it was public knowledge.''

Josie tried to smile, but it was more like gritting her teeth. ''I'm not following you, Fiona. You thought what was public knowledge?''

''That Beatrice Beaujold was…'' She lowered her voice and cleared her throat. ''A bit of a drinker.''

Chapter Six

SLOW-COOKED PORK CHOPS
(from page 132 of *The Way to a Man's Heart*
by Beatrice Beaujold)

These chops take hours to cook, which gives you a lot of time to find something else to do until they're ready. Stay in the vicinity of the slow cooker, and the scent will drive your man wild.

1 large red onion, peeled and sliced thin
salt and pepper, to taste
4 boneless pork chops, cut 1-inch thick
1 can or bottle of beer, room temperature

Put half the onions on the bottom of a slow cooker, then salt and pepper the pork chops and lay them on top of the onions.

Put the rest of the onions on top of the pork chops and pour the beer over everything.

Cook for 6 to 8 hours on low.

"But, you know," Fiona continued, "who isn't drunk at the cook-off? It's like a frat house around here."

Josie tried to arrange her features into an expression of surprise. "Where did you hear that about Beatrice?" It was her fault, Josie thought frantically. It probably had something to do with the papers she'd lost. Someone had found the letter—which could well have mentioned Beatrice's drinking—and was now spreading the news around town.

"Actually, I heard it from Harvey Lundquist, the pharmacist. He said he read it in the paper." Fiona shrugged. "It's probably just one of those rumors…who knows where they get started? I shouldn't have said anything."

"It was in the *paper?*" Her relief that the source of information might not be her lost papers was only fleeting. Had it really been published? Surely no newspaper had printed that kind of story about Beatrice. Someone from the agency would have let her know.

"That's what Harvey said. Isn't it true?"

Josie hesitated. "You know how it is, Beatrice is a favorite target of certain groups right now, so the rumors are flying."

Fiona looked dubious but said, "I can certainly

imagine that. That cookbook's got a lot of people mad, though personally I like it.''

''Oh? You have it?''

''Sure. Just made the pork chops for my neighbor yesterday.'' She hesitated. ''Come to think of it, I had a heck of a time trying to get him to leave.''

Josie laughed. ''I guess you have to be careful with that kind of thing.'' She changed the subject. ''Listen, I need to find some clothes quickly. The girl over at the Silver Moon Inn told me to go to a place called His Track, Her Rack. Can that really be true?''

Fiona laughed. ''It's true, all right. Bob and Shirl Watson couldn't agree on what kind of shop to buy when they came into some money, so they finally compromised and split one shop in two. Right down the middle. She sells clothes for women and he sells—''

''Auto parts.''

''Yup.'' She held up her right hand. ''Honest to God. But don't let that put you off. Shirl actually has some very nice stuff in there. She's got some pretty wild stuff, too, but don't let that put you off.''

''At this point, I'd settle for clean.'' Josie smiled. ''It was nice meeting you, Fiona.''

''Same here. I'm really sorry about what I said. I'm sure it's not true.'' Fiona turned the lock and pushed her door open. ''Wait.'' She reached in and took a small but elaborately iced cupcake from the display rack. ''Here. Maybe a little sugar boost for lunch will help you get going.''

''Thanks.'' Josie took the cupcake, said goodbye

to Fiona and hurried down toward Mulberry Street. Along the way, she ate the cupcake and it was delicious. Every bite exploded with the flavors of butter and vanilla. If she ever *was* to have a wedding this would be the place for it.

His Track, Her Rack was in a corner building of such ornateness that Josie almost walked right past it, thinking it was a bank. There was even a clock tower on the top, though it appeared to be stuck at six-thirty. According to Josie's watch—which she'd just spent far too much money on in a bid to look affluent in her new job—it was eleven-fifteen.

The bell on the front door jingled like wind chimes as she walked in, and almost immediately a small, dark-haired woman, wearing a tight red dress the exact color of her lipstick and high-heeled shoes, swooped over to Josie.

"Can I help ya?" She snapped her gum and smiled, showing teeth so gleaming and white that they had to be the work of a dentist.

"Yes, I need to get a few things to carry me through the weekend." Josie's eyes wandered over the unusual store. The front section was entirely women's clothes, everything from conservative linen skirts and high-necked white blouses to cut-away leather dresses and stilettos. The back half of the room, however, was a completely different world, with tires and large metal car parts Josie couldn't even begin to identify piled high on the floor and counter, and hanging on the walls.

"Well, you've come to the right place," the

woman said, extending a hand with inch-long crimson nails. "I'm Shirl Watson. I own the joint. Or at least—" she cast a derisive glance at the auto parts "—*this* side of it."

Josie shook her hand. "Josie Ross."

"You're not from around here, are you?"

"No. New York."

"Hotter than you expected here?"

Josie's mind flew to Dan. "I beg your pardon?"

"The weather? Is that why you need new clothes?"

"Oh, the weather…no, no. My suitcase was stolen, so all I have is what I'm wearing." She winced inwardly at the thought of the theft. And of the letter, whatever it said. And of the newspaper article.

"I see. Hmm." Shirl looked her up and down. "I think I've got some things that might suit you just fine." She led her around the store, pulling gorgeous clothes off the racks and piling them into Josie's arms. Her last stop was at the swimsuit rack, where she took out an impossibly tiny string bikini with a black-and-gold leopard print. "I'm guessing this isn't your style, but, honey, this would look spectacular on you."

Josie was about to decline, but something stopped her. She was tired of being predictable. "I'll try it on," she said, taking the bikini. It wasn't like she was going to actually *buy* it, but it would be fun to see how it looked.

"Great. Fittin' room's right over here." Shirl led her to a small room enclosed by sheets of drywall. "I've had a little trouble with the door lately, but if you close it really carefully and stand back, it should stay shut."

"Thanks." Josie stepped into the room and closed the door behind her. It swung right back open.

"See, that's what I mean," Shirl said. "Pull it real slow and firm and try not to stand on those front floorboards. When you step on them, the door goes loose. I've been pestering Bob to fix it, but for some reason he can't be bothered."

Josie tried again and the door stayed shut.

"So did you report your stolen suitcase to the police?" Shirl asked.

"I did, but they didn't seem that concerned." Josie lost her footing and stepped too close to the door. It started to swing open but she caught it. Maybe she was getting used to the way things worked around here, she mused.

"I can't believe they wouldn't care," Shirl said. "You should talk to the chief, Danny Duvall."

Danny? Her heart tripped. There was something sweet about that. Even if he was a bullheaded jerk. "He's the one I reported it to," Josie said, pulling on a pair of light linen pants.

"Yeah? And he hasn't found it for you yet? He's something of a legend around here. Some folks say he can apprehend a criminal with one hand while using the other one to…"

The bell on the door chimed, interrupting Shirl and leaving Josie to imagine what Dan would be doing with his other hand. Her mind reeled.

"Excuse me, honey," Shirl said. "Devil's here himself. You call me if you need anything."

Glad she could stop trying to make polite conversation for a few minutes, Josie quickly tried on the rest of the clothes Shirl had picked out for her. Without exception, they fit to a tee and flattered her coloring and shape more than she would have thought possible.

When she'd finished with the clothes, all of which made it into her "buy" pile, she eyed the bikini with some skepticism. It really wasn't her, and she absolutely didn't have time to try it on, but she just couldn't resist.

She shimmied into it and looked at her reflection in the mirror. She had to laugh. It did suit her. Or at least, it would suit someone who looked exactly like her but who had the nerve to go out in public practically naked.

She was just getting ready to take it off when she heard a familiar voice just a few feet away from the dressing room door.

"Ready yet, Bob? Guess I'm a bit early." It was Dan Duvall.

"Just a couple more minutes," Bob Watson answered. "Had some trouble screwing the rack back on because the metal was pulled out of shape."

Dan muttered something unrepeatable about the cook-off.

"I know it." Bob chuckled, then lowered his voice. "But the tourists aren't all bad. You didn't hear it from me, but there's one hot number trying on clothes over in Shirl's place right now.''

Shirl's Place. Like it was down the street.

''You're not suggesting I spy or anything, are you, Bob?'' Dan laughed.

Josie's mouth dropped open.

''Hell no, I'm just sayin' you might want to keep your eyes on the door because she's bound to be comin' out in a few minutes.''

''Who is it?''

''Dunno. Some out-of-town lady. Probably here for the cook-off.''

There was a derisive snort, presumably from Dan.

Josie frowned and moved closer to the door in order to hear better.

''Nah, this one's different,'' Bob was saying. ''Just introduced herself to Shirl, said someone stole her clothes. Joanne somethin'. Long wavy hair, figure that…well, trust me, she's gorgeous.''

Josie felt a flush of pleasure, despite herself.

''Joanne?'' Dan asked slowly. ''Or Josie?''

''Josie.'' There was the sound of Bob snapping his fingers. ''That's it.''

Josie held her breath, waiting for Dan's response.

She didn't hear it. Whatever his answer, it was obscured by the sound of a fire engine barreling past the window.

''She doesn't look like it to me,'' Bob said, sounding surprised, after the fire engine had rounded the corner and faded into the distance.

"Believe me," Dan said. "I can spot 'em a mile away."

Josie leaned closer to the door, forgetting about the floorboard, and it swung wide open before she could catch it.

That, in itself, happened silently. It was Josie's startled exclamation that drew their attention.

"What the—" Bob Watson looked at her and his eyes went wide.

Dan's expression also shifted for a moment to one of surprise. He was quick to regain his composure, though, and leaned against the counter. He raked his gaze over her and said, "Why, Ms. Ross. We were just talking about you."

"So I heard."

"You did?" Bob asked, glancing nervously at Dan.

Josie kept her gaze on Dan. "Most of it."

He didn't flinch. Didn't look embarrassed, or sorry for whatever it was he'd said about her that had surprised Bob so much.

"I would imagine," Josie went on, "that the chief of police would have better things to do than stand around gossiping about visitors to his town. Visitors, I might add, who bring necessary revenue into this place."

He gave a derisive laugh. "I could do without it, thanks."

She shook her head. "I'd think you'd be grateful, especially considering the fact that you're a civil servant whose job security and salary depend on the financial health of the city."

Bob held back a chuckle, making, instead, a loud snorting sound.

Dan flashed him a look, then said to Josie, "I appreciate your concern."

Shirl rounded the corner at that moment and clapped her hands to her cheeks. "Oh, my! It looks just *wonderful!*"

A split second of confusion passed before Josie simultaneously remembered what she was wearing and glanced down in horror to see just how much Dan and Bob Watson had been seeing.

"I was just going to say that," Dan said, noticing her horror and leaping on it. "Nice outfit."

Josie forced herself to keep her cool. "Thank you so much, Chief. Now, if only you could keep such a good eye on the criminals." Without waiting for a response, she turned and went back into the dressing room, slamming the door behind her. Naturally it bounced right back open, and she had to try again, more carefully. Then she leaned her back against it for a moment, hand on her chest, trying to still her pounding heart.

She *knew* she shouldn't have tried on the bikini. She may as well have been standing in front of him buck naked! In fact, she would have looked *less* provocative if she had been naked.

She hurriedly changed into a pale yellow slip dress, carefully removing the tag so she could pay for it with her other things. She was half tempted to add a jacket just so she would feel fully covered the next time she emerged from the dressing room, but she decided that would only make her more conspicuous. So she gathered up the clothes she was going to buy, and the tag from the dress she was wearing, and stepped back into the shop.

Dan was still there, talking with Bob at the counter. He turned and looked at her. "You changed your clothes," he said, a half smile playing at his lips.

"Yes, I decided this wasn't my style." She removed the bikini from the pile of clothes she set down on the counter for Shirl to ring up.

"I don't know," Dan said, leaning back against Bob's counter and assessing her from the short distance. "I thought it looked pretty good."

She couldn't help but smile. "Well…thank you."

"Better on you than it did on Peggy Wilkins, and that's saying something."

Oh, please. "Thanks."

"Then there was Rachel Lima." He looked off into the distance, remembering. "It looked pretty good on her."

Shirl, ringing up Josie's purchases, piped, "She did look good in it."

Josie was horrified to see that Shirl had chosen to stop and talk at the exact moment she was holding a silk thong that had been in Josie's pile.

Dan looked at it, then at Josie, with an expression that made her feel as if he'd ripped the thong off her himself. With his teeth.

"That's for me to wear with my cotton pants so I don't have a line," she said, feeling her face warm. This blushing was getting to be a constant thing around him. With any luck, maybe he'd just think she was sunburned. "Not that it's any of your business." Why had she said that? Why explain to him at all?

"I didn't ask."

"No, but you looked at me in a way that just begged explanation."

"Ms. Ross, if you can read my mind, we're both in a lot of trouble."

She hoped to heaven he couldn't see the flush that raced from her scalp, down her spine, to her toes. "I assume your mind is on your job and, specifically, on finding my stolen property."

"I don't think it is," Bob said, nudging Dan with his elbow.

Dan's eyes didn't leave Josie's. Her heart pounded in her throat.

"Bob Watson!" Shirl admonished. To Josie, she said, "That'll be $145.62."

Josie forced her attention back to Shirl, although she was achingly aware of Dan's eyes on her. She handed Shirl her credit card and asked him, "So. Is there anyone you haven't seen in that bikini?"

"Sure." .

"Ask him how many he's seen out of it," Bob said, before his wife swatted him on the shoulder and told him to shut his "big fat pie hole."

"You certainly spread yourself thin around here, don't you, Chief? Don't you have better things to do? Like track down criminals, for instance?"

He spread his arms in a broad shrug. "I have my nights off."

Josie's breath caught in her throat for a moment. She imagined he was more busy at night than he was during the day.

"So, you here for the cook-off?" Shirl asked Josie.

"Yes, actually, I am." She was glad for the distraction. "My company does publicity for Beatrice Beaujold, the cookbook author who's making an appearance here this year."

Shirl laughed. "Got your hands full with that one, huh?"

Dread coiled in the pit of Josie's stomach. "What do you mean?" It was the second time she'd asked it in an hour, but this time she had a terrible feeling she knew the answer. This kind of negative publicity on its own would be bad enough, but she had the sinking feeling that this *was* directly related to her stolen bags. Making the whole potential debacle *her* fault.

"That article on her in the *Chronicle* this morning was none too flattering," Shirl said. "Said she can really knock 'em back."

"The *Chronicle*," Josie repeated, panic mounting. It was true. Fiona had it right. Harvey the pharmacist had read it in the paper. And he was already spreading the tale, so even if Josie could somehow pick up every remaining copy of the *Chronicle* and throw it out, people were already talking. "That's just a local paper?"

"As local as it gets," Dan answered. "Never gets circulated outside Beldon."

Josie wasn't sure if he meant to be reassuring, but

she felt a modicum of relief, anyway. "Do you have a copy of it still?" she asked Shirl.

"No, sorry, honey. I lined the birdcage with it just before you came in here."

"I've got a copy of the article in the car," Dan said.

"You have it?" Josie asked, surprised.

"Well, yeah." There was an ace in his smile. "I figured it was potential evidence."

Wow. So he really hadn't dismissed her case entirely. "Were you going to tell me?"

He shifted his weight and regarded her lazily. "Why, Ms. Ross, aren't you Ms. Beaujold's PR agent? I would have thought surely you already knew about the article."

She swallowed a hot retort because, at the bottom of it all, he was right. She *should* have known. She should have been keeping up with the local paper and any coverage it might have of the cook-off and/or Beatrice's appearance. She just never would have dreamed this would happen. "Fortunately, I know now."

"So is the article right?" Shirl asked. "Does that Beaujold woman really..." She made a motion of lifting a bottle to her lips.

"No, of course not. Beatrice is..." She searched for something both flattering and true to say but came up short.

"A nutcase," Bob supplied.

All eyes turned to him.

"I beg your pardon?" Josie asked. Had he read the

newspaper article or—God forbid—did he have some other information?

"Yeah, a nutcase. She was in here last night buying a crowbar, and I can tell you she was up to no good. No good at all."

Chapter Seven

GUACAMOLE
(from page 99 of *The Way to a Man's Heart*
by Beatrice Beaujold)

If you're looking for a long night with your man, this spicy guacamole is just the fortification you'll need. Use a generous dash of cayenne pepper to warm the heart and other organs....

2 Hass avocados
1 small white onion, finely chopped
1 large clove garlic, minced
1 tomato, chopped fine
juice of one lime
dash cayenne pepper
salt and pepper, to taste

Peel the avocados, remove the pits and place the avocado meat in a shallow bowl.

Add the onion, garlic, tomato, lime juice, cayenne, salt and pepper, and mash together with a fork.

Chill for $1/2$ hour, then serve.

"A crowbar?" Dan repeated sharply. "Beatrice Beaujold was in here buying a *crowbar?*"

"You must be mistaken," Josie said, and meant it. Beatrice was too busy drinking at the inn to bother going out and buying tools.

Bob shook his head and pulled a copy of *The Way to a Man's Heart* out from under the counter. "Even gave me a signed copy of her book." He turned it over to look at the author's picture on the back. "That's her, all right."

"Bob Watson, what were you planning on doing with that book?" Shirl asked, her hands on her hips.

"Thought I'd give it to you, honey."

Shirl snorted.

"Back to the crowbar," Dan said. His face was still and serious. "Did she say what she wanted it for?"

"Said she needed it to pull out the oven racks," Bob said, scratching his head. "See what I mean? Nuts. You could just use tongs for that."

Shirl gave him a look of disbelief. "Like you'd know tongs if they pinched your—"

"Bob." Dan's voice was quiet but commanding. "Did she say anything else?"

"Hell, I don't know. She rambled on about needing protection or something."

Josie looked at Dan. "Do you think she bought the crowbar as protection against whoever pushed her down the stairs?"

"It's possible. Stupid, but possible."

"You don't think she's the one who messed up your car, do you?" Bob joked. "Maybe *you're* the one who needs protection. From *her!*" Clearly he thought this was hilarious.

Josie didn't. It was all too easy to believe.

The phone on Bob's desk dinged and he sobered enough to pick it up. He spoke quickly, then hung up. "Car's ready," he said to Dan, still chuckling. "You can get it around back."

"Thanks, Bob. I owe you one." Dan turned his gaze to Josie. "Need a ride back?"

"Actually, yes," Josie admitted. "And a look at that article." The hell with foolish pride; she had fires to put out. The drinking stories were bad enough, but what was Beatrice doing buying a crowbar from the auto parts store? None of this contributed one bit to the image Page-turner and Beatrice's publisher wanted for her.

Shirl handed Josie the charge slip and a pen, and she signed and gathered her bags.

"You want me to carry those for you?" Dan offered as they walked to the door.

"No, thanks. I've had enough of your commentary on my clothes for today."

He opened the door and stood back for her to go

through first. "Let me get this straight. You *don't* want my opinion?"

She couldn't help but laugh. "Although I understand you're a connoisseur, no, I don't."

They began walking toward the squad car on the south side of the building. "You just let me know if you change your mind."

She gave him a look.

He remained undaunted. "Just offering to help," he said, going to the passenger door and opening it in one expansive movement.

"How chivalrous."

She got in and reached over to close the door herself, but he beat her to it, then leaned down in the open window and repeated, "Don't let it be said that I'm not a gentleman."

"No one's going to hear it from me." She leaned back against the hot vinyl seat and breathed in the warm air. There was a faint, familiar scent in the car and it took her a moment to place it as Dan's soap, or shampoo, or detergent, or whatever it was that made him smell so good.

He got into the driver's seat and started the ignition. The engine roared to life. "You're a wise guy, you know that?"

Josie looked at him in surprise. "Me?"

He made a show of glancing around the car. "You're the only one here."

"I'm no wise guy," she argued, then turned to look at the street in front of them. "I just calls 'em as I sees 'em."

He gave a wicked smile and drew the car out onto the main thoroughfare. "You ain't seen nothin'. Yet."

A thrill ran through her, but she told herself it was because she wasn't used to driving so fast. In such a powerful car. With such a hunk of a man. She watched his hand, casually draped over the steering wheel, and marveled at how powerful even that looked.

She hadn't met a lot of men like this in the city.

"So where's the article?" she asked.

"Right here." Without taking his eyes off the road, he patted the seat next to him and pulled a thin newspaper out from under the atlas.

"Thanks," she said, taking it eagerly.

"Page three."

She turned to the right page and scanned for the article. It took a couple of moments because, fortunately, it was only a small item in the gossip section.

Nationally famous cookbook author, Beatrice Beaujold, who has written a cookbook on how to win a man's heart, is in Beldon for the Rocky Top Chili Cook-off. Sources close to the author say that she is the perfect candidate to take part in the brewery's activities, since she is in the habit of overindulging herself with the foamy stuff. It is further rumored that during her last appearance, at the Planko, Alabama, Renaissance Festival, she drank so much stout that she attempted to squeeze into King Henry VIII's armor for the jousting competition. The armor had to be removed by an engineer, resulting in a large bill for the Planko County Recreation Department.

Josie sighed and set the paper aside. "This is not good," she murmured.

"I'm just trying to figure out how she got stuck in Henry VIII's armor," Dan mused. "It's not like he was a small guy."

"Well, it's not like it was really his armor."

"Obviously, but you'd think they probably tried to be realistic, so it was probably a large suit of armor." Dan shrugged. "Not that it matters. There's nothing too damaging in there. Certainly there's nothing interesting enough for other papers to pick up."

"That's true," Josie said, hope lighting in her for the first time all afternoon. "Maybe it will just go away."

"Come Monday, I'm counting on it."

"That's right. By Monday this will all be over." She was counting the minutes.

But maybe, as he'd pointed out, this story would stay in this tiny little piece of real estate and no one else would ever hear about it. In fact, so many of the people who were here for the contest were drinking themselves, that they probably wouldn't even take the time to read the newspaper, much less that tiny little item, hidden in the middle pages.

Josie leaned back and looked over at Dan, watching his profile while he drove. Her mind traveled to places she would have preferred it hadn't. The man irritated the heck out of her, but she couldn't help but notice, and appreciate, the sensual curve of his mouth. And the dark shadow of a beard that made his eyes look that much bluer. And the unkempt tousle of dark, wavy hair that gleamed with health and gave Josie a sharp desire to run her hands through it.

As if reading her mind, he glanced over at her, and she felt naked all over again.

"What's the matter?" he asked, frowning.

"Nothing," Josie said, making an effort not to stammer. "I'm just worried about the time." She looked at her watch. It still read eleven-fifteen. She tapped the face of the watch but the second hand didn't budge. "What time is it?" she asked Dan.

He gestured toward the dashboard. "One-ten."

"Oh, no." So much for her restful moment. "I've got fifty minutes to try to get Beatrice to—"

"To what?" he asked, instantly on alert.

What was he so suspicious of?

She shook her head. "Nothing. Just…to perform. Her appearance fee was lost with my papers—you know, the ones you're supposed to be looking for?—and she told me earlier she won't fulfill her duties until she's been paid."

"I see." He nodded thoughtfully. "No wonder you were so snippy about everything last night."

"I was not snippy!"

He laughed. "And you're not now. Got it. Some folks just aren't good under pressure."

She gave an exasperated sigh. "Normally I'm *quite*

good under pressure. But things in your little town here don't seem to run normally.''

He pulled the car up to the curb outside the inn, put it into Park and looked at Josie. ''Funny, I've thought the same thing ever since you arrived.''

''Don't worry. I'm only here for three more days.''

He cocked his head. ''Something tells me it's going to be a long three days.''

''I'd lay money on it.'' She smiled and got out of the car, closed the door and leaned down in front of the open window. ''Thanks for the ride.''

He flashed her a grin. ''Anytime at all.''

She hurried into the lobby, flush with foolish excitement, only to have it doused the moment she saw Beatrice.

She was holding court on the sofa, just as she had been earlier, only this time there had to be at least ten empty beer bottles in front of her, along with a huge bowl of guacamole and chips.

''Beatrice,'' Josie said gregariously, holding out both her hands. ''Can I have a word with you? It's just about time to start.''

Beatrice shook her head obstinately. ''Can't do it.''

Josie sat next to Beatrice and leaned toward her, saying quietly, ''If it's about the fee, I have it right here.'' She opened her purse, took out her own checkbook and wrote out a check. That left her with about fifteen dollars in her checking account, she guessed, but at least it might save her job. Hopefully she wouldn't have to dip into her savings.

Beatrice watched her in silence, took the check,

folded it in half and dropped it into her cleavage. "It ain't the fee that's the problem, it's the baby." She punctuated this with a hiccup.

"The baby…?"

Beatrice nodded, her bleary eyes on Josie. "Cher left the baby with me."

Josie looked around, afraid to think where Beatrice might have stashed the infant. "Where is she?"

Beatrice hiccupped again. "Up in the room. I got this." She produced what looked like a walkie-talkie.

"Well, Beatrice, you're not supposed to be baby-sitting right now, you're supposed to be cooking one of your dishes, judging a preliminary round, then signing your books." Josie tried to sound patient, but she thought she could easily throttle the woman. "These appearances and your judging *must* be your priority this weekend."

"Cher paid me," Beatrice said, looking at Josie through hooded eyes. "Cash. More than I could say for you. Come to think of it, I should get that baby." She tried to stand up and fell back down.

Josie could just imagine the news articles—local or otherwise—if Beatrice Beaujold was seen baby-sitting an infant in this condition.

Josie pinched the bridge of her nose for a moment. She had a migraine coming on, she could feel it. It would probably last the rest of her life. "Okay, tell you what. I'll baby-sit until Cher gets back. You just stay here and have some coffee until it's time to make an appearance, okay?"

"I guess."

"Great." Josie looked at the clock on the wall. Beatrice was due in the kitchen in ten minutes. But she could conceivably be ten or fifteen minutes late without causing a problem. After all, cooking times were always variable.

Nearly half an hour of sitting quietly, drinking black coffee, might make her reasonably coherent.

Josie went to the coffeemaker on the sideboard and poured two cups for Beatrice, brought them both back and handed her one, setting the other on the table before her.

A woman came rushing up, pulling a reluctant-looking man. "Honey, you just *have* to try this. Really, it's the best I've ever had."

"I just ate five cinnamon crescents," he said, patting his stomach. "I don't think I have room for guacamole."

"Come on." She dipped a chip in and fed it to him. "Just one."

His eyes widened. "That *is* good."

She smiled smugly. "See? Now, wasn't there something you wanted to ask me?" She hooked her arm through his and led him toward the back door without acknowledging Josie or Beatrice at all.

"Idiot," Beatrice muttered.

"You know, Beatrice," Josie said, trying to steer the conversation to something that might sober Beatrice up. "You might sell a lot of books at this signing tonight. That's basically cash in hand."

Beatrice's eyes lit up, just as Josie suspected they would. "Yeah?"

"Oh, sure. Have you seen all the people here? You're the star attraction. If you have some coffee and…wake up a little more, you might be able to sign a whole bunch of books. Especially if you whet peoples' appetites with some delicious dish first."

"That's right, I could."

Josie nodded. "Good. You just enjoy your coffee for a few minutes and I'll go check on the baby."

Beatrice struggled to retrieve the monitor from the seat cushion behind her. "Here. Cher said if the baby cries you can hear it and see it on those little lights. I haven't seen or heard nothin'."

"Okay."

"Where are you off to?" Dan Duvall's voice came quietly from behind Josie.

She held up the monitor. "Baby-sitting."

"Really. I wouldn't have taken you for the type."

"Hello, there, sonny," Beatrice suddenly cooed at Dan. "How about you sit down and have a drink with me." She patted the seat cushion next to her. "Perhaps you'd like to try some of my delicious artichoke dip. I'm just off to the kitchen to make it now…."

Josie watched in disbelief for a moment. Beatrice actually appeared to be flirting with Dan Duvall. It was almost as unattractive as her barking at everyone. "Just make sure she keeps drinking coffee and *don't* let her fall down," she whispered to Dan as she walked past him. He could handle Beatrice's flirting however he wanted.

She started for the stairs, examining the blue-and-white walkie-talkie-like gizmo Beatrice had given her. Beatrice had said she'd be able to hear the baby and see the sound register on the LED. The fact that it was quiet and blank was good, then, wasn't it? Unless…she felt around the edges and found a little dial. The moment she clicked it, a scream emitted from the tiny speaker and the red LED readout blared. Josie nearly dropped the monitor in shock.

There followed a moment of quiet during which Josie told herself, as she hurried up the stairs, that the baby was probably settled and happy again.

Then she heard the slight shuddering intake of breath over the tiny speaker.

The second scream was even louder than the first and ended with a pitiful sob.

When she got to the room, the door was locked. She spat out an oath that would have had Sister Bernadetta in cardiac arrest.

''Something wrong?''

She whirled to see Dan, standing there looking as calm as could be.

Chapter Eight

GOLDEN ARTICHOKE DIP
(from page 19 of *The Way to a Man's Heart*
by Beatrice Beaujold)

There are a lot of stories about why artichokes are aphrodisiacs. I don't know what the truth is, but this dip can usually be relied upon to bring a man to his knees.

1 can artichoke hearts (not marinated)
1 cup mayonnaise
1 cup Parmesan cheese
few drops of Tabasco

Combine everything in a food processor and purée to a chunky-smooth consistency.

Bake at 400°F to golden brown and bubbly—about 20 minutes.

Serve on rounds of crusty bread or chips.

"It's locked," Josie said briefly. Another shrill cry sounded within. "I don't have the key." Her face and shoulders went icy. "Can you wait here while I go back to Beatrice and get the key, please?"

"You think that standing outside two inches of locked oak door while a baby screams hysterically on the other side really qualifies as baby-sitting?"

"Thanks a lot. Big help." She started to go.

Dan put a hand on her shoulder to stop her. "It's okay." He produced a gleaming brass key. "Right after you left, Ms. Beaujold asked me to come up and get her nerve tonic."

"Nerve tonic?" Josie repeated, watching anxiously as he opened the door.

He looked back at her, straight-faced. "She keeps it in a flask." With one sound click, the door swung open and Josie rushed in.

Britney lay silent, eyes closed, in her Portacrib. For one horrible moment, Josie thought she was dead. "Britney?" She laid a hand on the tiny chest and felt the rise and fall. "It's all right," she said, residual panic shaking her voice. "She's okay." She looked at Dan and felt a wave of gratitude that he was there.

He approached the crib and looked down at the sleeping child. "She's a lot cuter than her aunt," he commented, bending low for a closer look. He reached down and gently touched Britney's tiny hand with his large one.

Josie watched the callused thumb brush against the little palm, then looked at his face. He wore an expression of such tenderness that she thought, for a moment, that maybe—just maybe—he had a tender side she hadn't given him credit for.

"Do you have children?" she asked, hoping he wouldn't pull out the old *not that I know of* joke.

"No." His voice was only a whisper, and Josie braced herself for some emotional admission until he said, "I've gotta get a barefoot, pregnant wife first."

She sighed. She should have known it couldn't last. A man like this didn't make emotional admissions. Heck, a man like this probably didn't even *have* emotional admissions to make. A guy who was desired by probably every single woman in town didn't have time to get his heart involved.

Josie had to keep reminding herself of that.

"So why are you playing fetch for Beatrice?" she asked, trying to sound light.

He remained serious. "Let's just say I want to keep a close eye on her, and if I didn't come and get this for her, she'd come up herself."

"So?"

"So I can't very well keep an eye on her if she's in her room."

"Presumably if she's in her room, she's safe."

"Maybe. Then again, maybe everyone's safer if she's out in the open."

Josie frowned. "What are you talking about?"

"Just keep a good eye on her, okay?"

"You don't need to tell me how to do my job."

"Why not? You keep telling me how to do mine."

"That's because *yours* doesn't seem to be getting done!" she said in a harsh whisper.

Heat flashed in his eyes. "You think you could do better?"

She drew herself up, trying not to fall into the lure of those bright blue eyes. "Maybe I could."

They stood facing each other, eyes locked in silent challenge.

Then, slowly, Dan reached out and pulled her to him. "Then maybe I ought to deputize you."

She swallowed and looked into his face. It wasn't easy to keep her composure. "Maybe you should." Her voice was barely a whisper.

Another tense moment stretched between them before he gave a single, impatient shake of his head and lowered his mouth down onto hers.

She knew she should fight it, that she should draw back in outrage, but she couldn't, despite everything she'd just reminded herself about what a playboy Dan was.

Instead, she curled her arms around his shoulders and leaned into him, parting her lips in clear invitation to deepen the kiss.

He did.

When his tongue brushed against hers, it was as if a live wire touched the back of her neck and sent shock waves tingling down her spine. Reflexively, she pressed into him, tightening her arms around him.

They were heart to pounding heart, pressed together like welded metal.

This was crazy, Josie thought, running her hands through his thick, glossy hair. But she didn't want to stop.

Neither, it seemed, did Dan. He tightened his grasp around her lower back and she arched closer still. His badge was cold against her chest, even through the thin fabric of her shirt, reminding her of the powerful position he held in this town.

A reluctant thrill coursed through her, followed by another. If they didn't stop soon, she wasn't going to be *able* to stop.

A soft mewling from the baby had the effect of cold water being thrown on them.

"I forgot about her," Josie breathed, pulling back. Her face was flushed and she knew it.

What surprised her was that his was slightly flushed, too. "Some baby-sitter," he said with a laugh.

"It's not my primary occupation." She stepped back and straightened her clothes.

"Good thing." He hesitated. "Look, I'm sorry about that—" he gestured "—just now. I don't normally do that kind of thing."

"From what I gather, you're *always* doing that kind of thing." She tried to give a casual laugh, but it came out a little too hard. She didn't want him to apologize. There was something insulting about an apology for kissing someone.

His eyes narrowed, ever so slightly. Like Clint Eastwood's in *Dirty Harry.* "You gather wrong."

She shrugged. "Hey, tell your neighbors. They're the ones spreading tales."

"What's interesting is that you're listening."

He got her. "Only because there's nothing else to do around here."

"No? I'd have thought you'd have your hands full with your client." He gave her a sly smile, then went to the crib and looked down at the child. "So what's the baby's name?"

"Britney."

The baby stirred and started to cry.

Josie panicked.

Dan looked at her. "You gonna pick her up?"

"Of course. Unless…" She stopped. "You want to…?"

He eyed her.

The baby's cries grew stronger and Josie stiffened, afraid to make the wrong move.

Dan shook his head and went over to the crib. "Come on, baby," he said, in the same voice that had probably changed a thousand back-seat no's into yes's. Josie might have stepped forward herself if he hadn't reached down and picked Britney up and held her close against his broad chest. Almost immediately the baby stopped whimpering.

"Wow. You're pretty good with her," Josie commented softly. She knew exactly how that baby felt, folded into his arms. She felt safe and protected.

"She's just a baby—they're easy," he said, flashing his blue gaze Josie's way. "It's the grown ones that cause all the trouble."

"Maybe you're just nicer to babies than you are to full-grown women," Josie suggested, arching her brow.

"Babies don't talk back." He didn't wait for a response, which was good because Josie couldn't formulate one. "Here, I'd better get Ms. Beaujold's tonic and take it back downstairs."

"Oh. Okay." Josie made no move to take the baby, partly because she was afraid to get too close to him again, and partly because she didn't know how to hold the baby.

He waited for a moment, then said, "I'm thinking maybe you should take the kid."

She glanced at the content little form and knew, without a doubt, it would blow like Mount Vesuvius the minute she took it. "Why don't you just set her back in the crib?"

He looked at Josie for a moment, then, with the slightest shake of his head, set the baby down in the crib. "You afraid of babies?" he asked.

She watched as Dan gently lay Britney back on her white mattress. "Of course not. Why would you ask such a thing?"

He straightened up. "Because just now, when I asked if you wanted to take her, you looked like I'd drawn a gun on you. You're either afraid of her or me, and, judging from what just happened, I don't think it's me."

"What just happened," Josie said, trying to keep

her voice even, "was probably some kind of heat stroke." Lord knew it was hot in here.

He raised an eyebrow. "We didn't even make it to the stroking."

Josie swallowed hard. "The *baby*," she said pointedly, "has a schedule she must stick to. It's her nap time right now." She looked over to see two round blue eyes gazing at her.

"Okay, you're the expert." There was amusement in his voice. "I'd better get back to your friend downstairs before all hell breaks loose."

Privately, Josie thought it just had but she didn't say anything. She wasn't going to let Dan know he'd rattled her.

He stopped by the door and said, "I noticed some diapers over on the bedside table. You might want to give her a change. If it's in her schedule, I mean." His mouth eased into a half smile at what must have been a comical look of dread on Josie's face before he left.

"I'll do that," she said doubtfully. "No problem."

"Wish I could stay to see it," he said with a laugh. When he left he closed the door behind him softly, but the baby woke with a cry.

Josie let out a pent-up breath and collected herself. "Shh. It's okay," she said, trying to soothe from a distance of a couple of yards.

The baby's cries intensified.

"It's okay." She went over and touched Britney's leg tentatively. It was warm, and softer than she'd expected. "Hush, now."

When the crying didn't cease, Josie reached down and gingerly picked the baby up. She was much lighter than Josie had expected, and her tiny body shook with tension from the shrill cries. Josie's arms shook slightly. "It's okay, Britney, come on. Shh." She pulled the child in and folded her arms around her. The little bundle was surprisingly warm.

This wasn't so bad.

"Here we go." Josie began a bouncing walk around the small room. Softly, she sang the only song that she knew all the words to, an old Motown tune with a rousing beat. She continued humming the tune and bouncing around the room until the cries subsided into small whimperings, then, finally, sleep. Britney's tiny head rested against Josie's shoulder.

Emotion twisted in Josie's throat. She paused, her hand still on the baby's small back, and tried to quell the unexpected feeling. For years she had contended that she was not a maternal woman, that she was never going to have kids. And it was true, she couldn't imagine fitting a baby into her life. It wasn't that she didn't like children...really, she'd never known any very well. It was simply that she knew she wouldn't be able to give a child the time and attention necessary.

And, she had to admit, sometimes she felt as if she could barely take care of herself. How could she take care of a tiny, completely dependent baby?

However, a tiny mist of doubt hovered over her every once in a while, and, in the right mood, Josie occasionally questioned her priorities and the direction her life was taking. Only half joking, she liked to blame a masseuse she'd used in a New Mexico hotel during a writer's conference five years ago. She'd wrenched her back carrying boxes of books to a literary signing and had employed the services of Magda, a massage therapist from the hotel spa.

Before becoming a masseuse, Magda had made her living reading people's auras. Apparently the money wasn't all that great in aura reading. Anyway, ten minutes into her massage, Magda asked Josie if she'd ever lost a child. When Josie told her no, she seemed surprised and told her that there was a small soul attached to hers, waiting for the opportunity to join her on earth. Usually that happened with women who had miscarried, Magda said, when the baby was waiting for a better time to be born.

Normally Josie didn't believe in fortune telling, aura reading, ghosts, clairvoyance or any other supernatural phenomena. She was a logical woman; she understood that fortune tellers knew what to say to gain trust and to make a gullible person believe them.

But Magda's words had stayed with her, humming on a very low frequency for five years, so that every once in a while they came back to her, making her question the choices she'd made, the choices she continued to make. Did she really want to forgo the experience of having her own family? In twenty or thirty or forty years, would she feel differently? Would she regret the decision to make work her priority? Would success in her job be satisfaction enough?

It was now. But would it always be? She didn't

know how to even think about it. Meanwhile the chances fell from her every month like sand from an hourglass. If she did nothing about it, biology would make the decision for her, permanently, irretrievably.

Of course, there was another variable that she hadn't even touched upon. In order to have a baby, she needed a man. Not just a sperm donor, but a good, honest, strong, Boy Scout of a man to be a father. Babies needed both voices in their lives. Britney's reaction to Dan Duvall had proved that. She'd been lulled by the deep voice, comforted by the strong arms.

"In the future you'll have to watch out for men like him," Josie warned in a singsongy voice, holding the baby close. "He may be all right to sleep on when you weigh twelve pounds, but you wouldn't want to date him when you're older, believe me. I don't know why, but guys like that always get lucky in the gene pool. Nice eyes, sexy mouth, hard body, great voice." She sighed. "Everything they need to lure foolish women into their beds. And there are plenty of foolish women who are willing to go with them." She shook her head. "Not me. Yes, he caught me at a weak moment in here, but I won't make that mistake again. And I *certainly* wouldn't allow it to go any further than it did." *Liar,* her inner voice chided. If there hadn't been a baby in the room, three more seconds of Dan's kissing and she would have forgotten everything she was here to do.

In fact, she was having a hard time keeping her mind on her job, anyway. Something about that kiss and this small baby in her arms combined to conjure up unexpected fantasies of domesticity in Josie's mind. Maybe *fantasies* wasn't the right word, because this didn't feel like any ordinary daydream. It was more like…premonition.

Suddenly Josie had a very clear vision of herself living in one of those grand old Southern houses on Main Street, holding the baby in a rocker on the front veranda, waiting for Dan to walk home from the station in the evening to join them for dinner.

She also had a clear vision of herself and Dan later, in the bedroom, lying together as the warm summer breeze blew lace curtains….

She stopped herself. This was crazy. She didn't have some dreamy Ward-and-June-Cleaver future with Dan Duvall. She barely even knew him!

So why did it *feel* so much like she knew him?

Before she could conjure an answer for that one, the door opened and Cher slunk in.

"That Britney?" she asked, incredibly.

Josie swallowed a smart retort. "Well, yes, Cher, it is."

"You baby-sitting?"

Josie hesitated, looking for some sign of humor in Cher's eyes, but she saw none. "Your aunt had some work to do downstairs and you weren't around so I had to come up to wait with the baby until you came back. Which you have now, so I'm going back downstairs." She carried Britney to Cher and carefully pried her off. "She needs a change," she added with some authority.

Cher took her with surprising tenderness. "Thanks," she said.

"All right, then," Josie said, "I'm going back downstairs now." Then she added, with an unaccustomed protectiveness, "You take good care of that baby."

"I do," Cher snapped. Apparently this wasn't the first time someone had cast doubts on her capability.

Five minutes later, Josie was picking her way through a kitchen crowded with test stoves and contest cooks. At first, she didn't see Beatrice, and for one uncomfortable moment she imagined her passed out somewhere. Then she saw Dan across the room in front of a wide, bright window, and noticed the bushy top of Beatrice's gray head several feet away from him.

"How's everything going?" Josie asked, approaching them.

"They haven't got any Duke's mayonnaise in this town," Beatrice bitched.

"Won't another mayonnaise do?"

"Not much of a cook, are you?"

Josie felt Dan's eyes on her, waiting for an answer that would further confirm his ideas about city girls. "I cook," she protested feebly. "Some." She saw another brand of mayonnaise on the counter. Obviously it didn't make that much of a difference, since she was using a different brand.

Beatrice snorted and thrust a block of cheese and a grater into Josie's hands. "Then help out, girlie. Grate a couple…three cups of that for me." Without waiting for a response, she turned back to an artichoke she was butchering on the counter.

Josie hesitated. Did she want two cups or three? And where was a measuring cup? All she had was a glass bowl.

Dan scraped a stool across the floor and sat down next to Josie as she timidly began running the cheese across the grater. He watched her in silence for a few minutes, which made her nervous. Her hands shook a little.

"Need help?" he asked.

"No, thanks. I can grate cheese."

"My guess is you're more used to having a waiter in a penguin suit hover over your plate and do it for you."

He was absolutely right. Except about the penguin suit. "Most waiters don't wear tuxes anymore."

He laughed. At her, she knew. Not with her. "I don't get out much."

That, she knew, was debatable. "I don't know, Chief, if the women around here are to be believed, it sounds as if you get out quite a bit."

He gave half a smile. "What's the matter, you jealous?"

The cheese chose that moment to slip from her grasp and she ran her thumb along the grater while the Parmesan thunked onto the counter.

"Ouch!" She raised her thumb to her mouth for a moment, then examined the wound. It throbbed, but it didn't look too bad.

"Told you," Beatrice smirked. "Not much of a cook."

Dan was off the stool and in front of her in an instant. "Let me see it," he said, taking her hand gently in his.

"It's not that bad," she protested, trying to pull her hand back. She'd already proved—to herself and to him—that she was vulnerable to his touch.

"Just let me see." He looked closely at it while she stood there, feeling stupid and tingly all at once. "That's not too bad."

"That's what I said."

"Well, you're right. Let's clean it up and put a bandage on it and you'll be good to go." He looked around. "There should be a first aid kit at every cooking center in here."

"That won't be necessary," Josie said. "You really don't need to trouble yourself."

He found the kit and opened it. "What, and just let you bleed all over the food? Forget it. I love artichokes. I want to try this stuff when it's done." Would it draw him irresistibly to Beatrice, Josie wondered with an inner smile at the thought.

"Let's have the thumb."

She couldn't help smiling. "Sure you wouldn't prefer another finger?"

"Very funny. Now, come on."

She kept her hand back like a selfish child. "I'll do it myself."

"Nah. I have a better angle. Besides, I feel kind of responsible."

"How so?"

He dabbed an alcohol pad on her cut. "Obviously you were rattled when I asked if you were jealous of the women I've dated."

Josie's mouth dropped open. "Are you joking?"

"Now, now, there's nothing to be embarrassed about." He took a Band-Aid out and unwrapped it.

"You're incredible."

He stopped long enough to give her a brief pirate's smile. "If I had a dime for every time I heard that…"

She groaned.

"Hold still." He wrapped the bandage around her finger, then let go. "You're done." He indicated the hand that she was still holding out toward him.

She snatched it back. "Thanks." She retrieved the block of cheese, knocked a scrap of paper off of it and resumed her grating.

"The problem is you're pushing too hard," Dan said.

"*I'm* pushing too hard? You're the one who said I'm jealous, which—have I mentioned?—I'm not."

He smiled. "The cheese. You're pushing it too hard against the grater. That's why you lost control. In this instance."

She bristled at his implication.

"You don't like being out of control, do you, Ms. Ross?"

She didn't answer, she just continued grating, harder than ever.

"If you give it a chance," he continued, undaunted

by her lack of reaction, "you might actually find you like it."

"Like what?" she asked. "Being out of control?"

"Just easing up a little." He stepped behind her and leaned forward, placing one hand on each of hers. "Easy," he said, guiding her movements. "Like this." He ran her hand back and forth, back and forth, across the grater.

Josie wanted to fight him, but she was too busy fighting an impulse to lean back against him and languish in the safety of a man's arms for a moment. "I can do it," she said.

"Easy," he repeated, in slow molasses tones. "See?"

He was right, it did work better his way. "Yes, I've got it. Slow, easy, light. It's not brain surgery."

"Thank God." He chuckled and backed off.

Part of her was sorry. She kept grating, looking for something to say. Outside, sirens blared in the distance. "You do a lot of cooking, Chief Duvall?"

He sat back on the stool and watched her work.

"Woodworking," he said. "Same motion."

"Oh." It figured the small-town, Southern, he-man police chief did woodworking.

The sirens outside grew louder.

Dan frowned and looked out the window.

"What's taking you so long with the cheese?" Beatrice barked, startling Josie so much that she nearly dropped it again. "Dump all this in the blender and mix it up." She thrust a bowl of artichoke hearts and a jar of mayonnaise at Josie.

Josie was about to give Beatrice a heated lecture on how she wasn't a slave and Beatrice would catch more flies with honey than with vinegar when a long fire truck raced past the window and stopped next to the inn itself.

Not a moment later, someone threw open the kitchen doors and cried, "Fire!"

"Where?" someone asked.

"In the display room. Someone set the entire stack of Beatrice Beaujold's cookbooks on fire."

Chapter Nine

CINNAMON CRESCENTS
(from page 19 of *The Way to a Man's Heart*
by Beatrice Beaujold)

Cinnamon is one of the surest aphrodisiacs there is.
If you're in a hurry, make these sweet rolls and
watch your man beg for more.

1 tube (8 oz.) refrigerated crescent rolls
1/4 cup butter, melted
cinnamon-sugar
4 large marshmallows

Spread the crescent rolls out on the counter, pinch
perforations closed to make solid sheets and cut the
solid sheets into 4 squares.

Spread each square with butter, then top with cinnamon-sugar.

Put 1 marshmallow in the middle of each square, pull the dough over the marshmallow and pinch the seams shut.

Bake at 375°F until golden brown (about 10-12 minutes).

Josie dashed out of the kitchen, but Dan stopped to grab the fire extinguisher from the chrome shelf that held all the appliances. The extinguisher was so dusty it looked pink instead of red, but it didn't appear as though it had been used before, so Dan hoped it would still work.

A crowd had gathered around the smoldering pile of books, and Dan had to push people aside to get to it. By the time he did, Josie was throwing glasses of water, lemonade and whatever else people handed her in order to put it out. Every time she moved, she got perilously close to the flames.

"Step aside," Dan ordered, putting an arm out to move her back. She wouldn't like that, he knew, but he didn't give a damn if it would help keep her safe.

As soon as Josie was out of the way, he pulled the safety pin on the extinguisher and pressed the release button. The flames died almost instantly in a cloud of white powder.

Everyone stood in silent shock for a moment, until the front door crashed open and four firemen in full regalia tramped in, lugging a long fire hose.

"It's out, guys," Dan said.

One of them lifted his visor and swabbed his forehead with the back of his arm. "Dammit, Danny, do you always have to get there first?"

Dan followed his gaze to the fire extinguisher in his arms and laughed. "What can I say? You guys are too damn slow."

Some good-natured ribbing followed, ending with Dan suggesting the fire chief might want to send an investigative team out to try to figure out what happened.

"You don't think it was an accident?" Chris Little, a volunteer fireman and high school coach, asked.

"I'm pretty sure it wasn't."

A collective gasp sounded from the onlookers.

"Wait a minute, Chief," Josie said, clutching his arm hard. "Didn't you tell me that this kind of thing happens all the time during the cook-off?" She didn't wait for an answer, but instead addressed the crowd. "Chief Duvall was just this afternoon telling me what a hard time they have with pranksters this time of year. Why, earlier someone pulled the emergency light off the top of his car." She shook her head sympathetically and patted Dan's shoulder. "The civil servants and volunteers of Beldon put up with an awful lot so that we can enjoy this chili cook-off. How about we all give them a hand?" She began to clap and the crowd followed suit.

Next thing he knew Dan was standing in the middle of an ovation, with Josie smiling pointedly in a silent plea for him to keep quiet about anything negative that had to do with Beatrice Beaujold.

He could understand why she felt that way, but he didn't have any intention of jumping through hoops to hide investigations so that Josie's client could look good.

"That's enough." He held up his hands to stop the applause. "I'm sure the fire department appreciates your…appreciation…but this is now the scene of an investigation, so I'm going to have to ask you all to leave."

"Please," Josie said. "Help yourselves to some of Beatrice Beaujold's famous cinnamon crescents, which you'll find by the kitchen."

Dan looked around, surprised to see that Beatrice Beaujold herself was nowhere to be seen. Why hadn't she come to see the commotion when everyone else did? Especially considering the fact that it was her books that were on fire.

He scanned the crowd, then caught sight of her alone in the other room, sipping a beer and smoking a cigarette. She wasn't even looking in the direction of the fire. She was just looking off into space, smoking and drinking.

Dan was about to go question her when Jerry showed up, pushing his way through the crowd. "Is there something we should know, Chief Duvall?" He reached for a pen over his ear, then patted his back pocket, sighed and put the pen back. "Is there cause for alarm?"

"Only the five-alarm chili some of the contestants are making," Josie chirped desperately.

Dan had to hand it to her. She was just trying to do her job, but damned if she wasn't adorable when she was flustered. And there was no doubt about it, she was flustered.

The question was, why? Was she just worried about her client? Or did she know more than she was saying?

"No cause for alarm," Dan said, waving the remaining stragglers away. "But I have to ask you to leave so that the evidence isn't disturbed."

"Not that there's evidence of anything sinister," Josie added quickly.

Slowly the remainder of the crowd dispersed while Dan watched, feeling Josie's glare on him until he finally turned to face her. "Something wrong?"

"You didn't have to announce there was an investigation!" she rasped.

"There *is* an investigation," he countered.

"Well, I'm glad to hear it, don't get me wrong, but I don't think you needed to tell the entire public that. All you're going to do is create panic."

"And possibly call less-than-flattering attention to your less-than-sterling client?"

Josie's face went pink. "What gives you the right to make judgment calls about my client or anyone else?"

"Hey." He smiled. "I just calls 'em as I sees 'em."

She recognized his reference to her own words and

gave him a dirty look. "If *anything* happens to Beatrice because of your shining a big spotlight on this, I'm holding you personally responsible."

"Has it occurred to you that if the person causing all this trouble knows there's an investigation, he or *she*—" he paused significantly, but Josie didn't react "—is more likely to stop?" A quick glance told him that Beatrice Beaujold was still in the other room, only now she was surrounded by people holding out books for autographs. Good. That would keep her busy for a while. "You should be thanking me."

Josie pinched the bridge of her nose for a moment before responding. "On the other hand, maybe you've just called *more* attention to their pranks so they can garner a *bigger* audience and plan something even *worse*. Something that may seriously injure Beatrice."

He nodded slowly. "That's possible. But unlikely."

"Really?" She was clearly angry. Oddly, it was a look that suited her. So far he hadn't seen a look that *didn't* suit her.

For the second time that day, he wanted to take her into his arms and kiss her senseless.

He had to get control of these insane impulses. They could only lead to trouble.

"And just how do you know that?" she asked.

He hesitated, collecting his thoughts and his libido before telling her the one thing he knew she didn't want to hear. "Because I think Beatrice Beaujold herself might be the one pulling the pranks."

* * *

Josie grabbed Dan by the arm and dragged him into the isolated hallway next to the display room. "Could you *please* keep it down if you're going to say something like that?"

He looked at her hand on his forearm, then at her. "Is this a pass?"

She drew her hand back as if she'd touched a snake. "No. If I made a pass at you, Chief, you'd know it."

"Like earlier?"

"I believe it was *you* who made an advance on *me* earlier," she said, trying to maintain her composure in the heat of remembering their kiss. "And I also believe you're trying to change the subject. Now, tell me what on earth makes you think Beatrice is behind any of this. I mean, for Pete's sake, she was with *us* in the kitchen when the books caught on fire. How could she have set it?"

"She could have had someone do it. Her niece, maybe. Or someone else."

"Come on. Why would she do that?"

He shrugged. "It's not my job to psychoanalyze criminals. Only catch them."

"First, I object to you characterizing Beatrice as a criminal, and second, it's insane that you would even think that. It's—it's irresponsible of you. It's *incompetent.*"

Dan remained unperturbed. "Did you notice she didn't leave the kitchen when the books caught on fire?"

Josie frowned and glanced around. "No. But that doesn't mean anything. Maybe she was afraid to come in, for fear that someone was after her." In which case, Josie never should have left her, she thought with guilt.

Dan shook his head. "She's been right in there the whole time. Facing the other way. Smoking a cigarette and drinking a beer."

Josie followed his gesture to see Beatrice holding court among a group of fans. "There you go. She *did* come to see what was going on. She only kept her distance. I think it's quite sensible."

"What about the crowbar?"

She knew exactly what he was asking, but she didn't have a snappy comeback for that one. "Crowbar?"

He cocked his head. "The one she bought from Bob Watson? What does a cookbook author who's come to sign books and make fussy little appetizers need with a crowbar?"

"I don't know. Did you ask her? Maybe she needed it for the jack in her car." Josie threw up her arms. "Who knows? Are you suspicious of everyone who's bought a crowbar this week?"

"Yes."

"Then why aren't you out chasing those leads? Why pick on Beatrice?" She took a short breath. "You know, she might have been killed when she was pushed down the stairs. Do you think she did that herself, too?"

"I think she might have."

Josie gaped at him in disbelief.

"There were no witnesses. The one person, other than you, who was on the scene around the time of that incident reported that Beatrice was the only other one in the hall."

"So did you question that person?"

"Of course. But Father Laraby has very good character references."

The clock in the hallway chimed the half hour. "I've got to go," Josie said, turning on her heel. "Beatrice was supposed to start signing half an hour ago."

"Make sure she doesn't leave the premises, would you?"

She whirled back to face him. "Chief Duvall, I hope that's a joke."

His expression softened. "Just keep an eye on her. I don't want anyone to get hurt. Including you."

What could she say to that? Thank him for his concern, or chastise him for his lack of concern? The whole thing was a mess.

But it was clear that she, herself, was going to have to keep close tabs on Beatrice. And it wasn't going to be easy.

Ten minutes later, Josie had managed to set Beatrice up at a makeshift display table in the lobby and had organized the crowd of fans into an orderly line. She'd salvaged most of the books from the other room, although they smelled a little smoky. Fortunately they'd still been in unopened boxes and Dan had relented and let her have them.

Satisfied that at least something seemed as if it was going to go right, she stepped back and watched the proceedings. Every once in a while she stole a glance at the clock on the wall and calculated just how long it would be until she could finally conk out on her bed and get some much-needed sleep.

"Hey," a voice said softly in her ear.

She turned around to see Dan.

"Recognize this?" he asked, opening his pocket to reveal a flash of flowered nylon, which she recognized as a bra she'd bought in Hawaii a few months ago.

She gasped. "Yes! Did you find my suitcase? And did you rifle through it?" Seeing her underwear in his pocket, knowing he had handled it, *seen* it, made Josie feel exposed. "Let me have that back."

Without thinking, she reached into his pocket and pulled it out, along with a half a pack of Wint-O-Green Life Savers.

He took the Life Savers back and offered her one.

She shook her head.

He popped one in his mouth. "No, we didn't find your suitcase. In fact, this was all there was. It was in a tree way out on the back lawn. My men didn't see it last night in the dark, but one of them found it this morning."

Under normal circumstances, she would have been horrified that her underwear was hanging from trees, but these weren't normal circumstances. At all. "Was there anything else?'' she asked hopefully. ''Papers? Beatrice's check? A letter addressed to me?''

He shook his head. ''This is it. But don't worry, they're still out there looking.''

It was probably just exhaustion, but for a moment, Josie just wanted to give it all up and quit. The odds against her succeeding this weekend, with both Beatrice and her job intact, seemed overwhelming.

But Josie wasn't a quitter. She wasn't going to give up, no matter how challenging things got.

And they were. The book signing seemed to go on forever. People had an endless variety of questions for Beatrice, from what kind of wine to serve with filet mignon—to which her answer was that she didn't eat that fancy steak and if it didn't go with beer it wasn't worth having—to how best to seduce a man who hadn't yet determined his sexuality—to which her answer was unrepeatable and probably shouldn't have been said in public in the first place.

Josie spent three hours of the book signing on guard, lurching forward every now and then to smooth over one of Beatrice's snippy answers.

At a couple of minutes past five, Josie was about to announce that the signing was over, when someone raised a hand and asked Beatrice how she protected herself from rabid fans.

Josie watched in horror as Beatrice crossed her legs, revealing—only to Josie—a small handgun strapped to her thigh.

''I ain't met one yet I couldn't lick in a fight,'' Beatrice said, patting her thigh.

Immediately, Josie stepped between her and Dan so he wouldn't see the gun.

"What are you doing?" he whispered.

"Just getting ready to wrap this up," she answered, her heart pounding in her ears. If he saw that gun and Beatrice didn't have a license to carry it, there was no telling what he'd do. Already this morning he'd told some poor old woman she couldn't sell her crocheted hats.

"She have any other appearances tonight?" Dan asked.

"No." Josie's shoulders sagged. With any luck she could bundle Beatrice up to her room and settle her in front of the TV with a case of beer. Let her drink herself into a stupor. Josie didn't care. As long as she wasn't here, talking to people, sipping from that infernal flask.

"What about you?"

She looked at him. "What about me?"

"Are you planning to stay in your room tonight?"

"Are you propositioning me?"

"No."

Something like disappointment settled in her chest. "So what do you care where I go?"

"I'm not convinced you're entirely safe yourself."

This was something that hadn't even occurred to her before. "You mean from whoever's trying to hurt Beatrice?"

His mouth went grim. "Yeah. Or…whatever."

She knew what he meant. "Or her."

He shrugged and shifted his weight from one leg

to the other. ''I'm just asking what your plans are for tonight.''

Josie moved to make sure she blocked his line of vision to Beatrice. ''Don't worry, Chief, I'll be here, tucked away in my bed, safe and sound.'' She looked at the clock on the wall. Five-fifteen. She wanted this day to end. ''In fact, I plan to turn in early.''

''That's good news,'' he said, shifting again.

She moved again.

Their arms bumped.

''What are you doing?'' Dan asked her.

She gave him a blank look. ''Nothing. I just told you, I'm getting ready to close this up and go on to bed.''

He eyed her suspiciously for a moment, then took a deliberate step to the side.

She watched him, decided that he'd stepped in the wrong direction to see Beatrice, and stood steadfast. ''Any more questions?'' she asked innocently.

''Yes, I have one,'' a voice said from behind her.

Josie turned to see Buffy stepping forward out of the crowd with her hand raised. ''Ms. Beaujold, would you characterize the effect of your recipes as magic or witchcraft?''

There was a glint in Buffy's eye that Josie hadn't noticed previously. Her voice was almost accusatory. Josie wondered if something had happened with Buffy and her fiancé between last night and this afternoon.

''I don't know 'bout witches, but my mama always called it the *gift*,'' Beatrice answered. ''Most of the women in my family have it. I say *most* because my sister's useless with it, but nearly all the other women can do it.''

The crowd laughed, much to Josie's relief.

In the back of the room, there was a *clunk* sound and a large potted plant fell over. Josie barely gave it a glance, but Dan slipped through the crowd and was there in a matter of seconds.

Josie watched with curiosity.

Meanwhile, Buffy continued her question, ''Does that mean that the recipes only work for people who also have that gift?''

Beatrice leaned back in her chair and Josie could tell she was just itching for a beer and a cigarette so she could hold court on this subject. ''Well, now, I wouldn't say that. If you follow the recipes exactly, they should have the desired effect. But if you go trying to get fancy or try to go one better on them— that's one of the mistakes my sister made—they won't work.''

''What if two women try the recipes on the same man?'' Buffy asked.

Josie frowned. What was she getting at?

''Lucky man'' was all Beatrice said, with a snort of laughter. ''Any other questions?''

Buffy's hand shot up, but Beatrice looked as if she didn't see her.

''You there in the back,'' Beatrice said, pointing like a stern grade school teacher.

''Are you planning to do any more cookbooks?''

''Oh, I could do a million of 'em.''

Josie made a mental note never to be tricked into accompanying Beatrice on tour for any of those million other books. In fact, if it was that or lose her job, she was seriously starting to think she'd rather pump gas for a living.

"It doesn't look like she's giving up any time soon," Dan commented when he returned. More hands shot up and Beatrice began pointing and answering.

Josie sighed. "It certainly doesn't."

"Can I have a private word with you?" he asked.

Josie glanced back at Beatrice, who was uncrossing her legs, once again revealing a small steely glint. It would probably be best to get Dan out of here for now.

"Sure," she said. "Where to?"

He led her to a door in the back of the building and outside onto the wide veranda. He motioned for a lone officer on guard to move to the front of the building.

"I don't want to leave Beatrice for long," Josie said, drinking in the thick scent of honeysuckle and wishing she could sit down on a chaise longue and rest for a few days.

"She'll be safe in there." He went to a table where someone had set up an icy pitcher of lemonade and about twenty untouched glasses.

"I'm not worried about her being in danger," Josie said. "I'm worried about what she might say. Or do. Or both."

"She's doing all right," Dan said easily. He poured

two glasses and gave one to Josie. "Those people love her." He gave a laugh. "I can't tell you *why*, but they do."

"I guess the recipes must work." She took a sip of the lemonade. Then another. It was tart and sweet and delicious.

"That artichoke stuff was good."

"I didn't have time to try it. It smelled great, though," she said, drinking some more lemonade. She'd had a late breakfast and no lunch at all.

"You want more of that?" he asked, looking at her empty glass.

Josie raised an eyebrow. "I don't know. Is it from Beatrice's book? You wouldn't be trying to take advantage of me, would you?"

"No." He didn't move closer, but the way he looked at her made her feel as if he had. "Why?" he drawled deliberately. "Are you suddenly finding me irresistible?"

Actually, yes, but it wasn't sudden. "Not at all." Josie's breath caught on the last word.

"Not even a little?" He looked into her eyes and she nearly gasped at the intensity focused on her from his own pale gaze.

"I'm not sure I know what you mean," she said, losing control of the conversation with every breath she took.

"I'm pretty sure you do." He slid his hand down her forearm, grasped her wrist and pulled her toward him.

It was difficult to get the words out. She set the

glass down. "I think I've had enough of this," she said, immediately kicking herself for such a stupid comeback. It was his eyes, she decided. He was hypnotizing her. There was no other explanation for why she was becoming such a babbling idiot around him.

"I'd love to see what you could do with a good cut of meat." He bent and brushed her cheek with a kiss. It felt hot where his lips touched her. He kissed her other cheek, then nuzzled down against her neck.

She leaned her head back and trembled with pleasure as he brushed tiny kisses all along the sensitive skin in the hollow of her throat. "I don't eat meat," she said weakly.

He only laughed in response, his breath hot against her neck.

"I'd better get back inside," Josie said, but she didn't move.

"Definitely," he said, but he didn't let go of her.

"If anyone sees us, it could be a lot of trouble for both of us."

He moved to her ear and said softly, "I think we're already in trouble."

Chapter Ten

STEAK FINGERS
(from page 78 of *The Way to a Man's Heart*
by Beatrice Beaujold)

Rare is the man who can resist fried meat. Add a
little extra-spicy Old Bay seasoning, or cayenne
pepper, to turn up the heat in your relationship.

1 lb. round steak
2 eggs
$^1/_2$ cup milk
salt and pepper, to taste
Old Bay seasoning, to taste, or cayenne pepper
1 $^1/_2$ cups flour
$^1/_2$ cup oil

Pound the steak with a tenderizing mallet, then cut into strips.

Combine eggs, milk, salt, pepper and Old Bay in a shallow bowl and whisk.

Dip steak strips in egg mixture, then in flour, and shake off excess and repeat.

Fry in hot oil for two minutes, or until golden brown.

His words sent shivers across her skin, down her neck and shoulder.

Trouble was right. She could hardly find her voice. "I don't need any more trouble."

He nibbled at her earlobe. A tingle wound its way down her spine and settled deep in her pelvis, throwing her needs—for trouble and other things—into chaos.

"Maybe you do. Maybe we both do." He trailed kisses across her jawline and stopped at her chin, as if waiting for her response.

He didn't have to wait long; she was anxious to quell her aching need and her lips sought his. The instant they met, she felt a rush of adrenaline course through her.

She needed more, and more.

He met her fervent desire with his own. When his tongue touched hers, the electricity intensified. She drank in the taste of him, breathed the clean scent of his skin, dissolved in his firm embrace.

She didn't want this to end. She almost didn't even care if someone saw them. If this all came of a kiss, making love with him would probably be unbearable.

And if they kept this up for long, not making love would be unbearable.

"We can't do this," Josie murmured, pulling back.

"Why not?" He pulled her close again and kissed the sensitive skin by her ear. His voice was soft and husky; it sent shudders through her.

Because I have no self-control. If we keep doing this, I won't be able to stop. "Because we're both supposed to be working." It hardly seemed a sufficient reason at this point.

"You're right," he conceded, stepping back as if coming out of a spell. "Of course. I shouldn't have done that."

Josie straightened her clothes and tried to make her breathing normal again. "Maybe there's something in the lemonade," she said with a laugh. "Or those steak fingers they were passing around earlier."

"Leave the Freudian psychology at home," Dan said, looking at her steadily. "You don't need magic recipes to make sparks fly between two people."

If he kept talking like that, she was going to throw herself into his arms and kiss him again, or melt into a little puddle of feminine idiocy right there on the flagstone patio.

She didn't think either of those things would be very good for her professionalism.

"What was it you wanted to talk to me about?" she asked. "I assume it wasn't…" She gestured.

"No, it wasn't. Wait here a minute." He went down the steps to a squad car that was parked several yards away. When he came back he was holding a radio out to her. "I think you should hold on to this over the weekend."

"What's this?" she asked, taking it. "A walkie-talkie? Wow, I haven't seen one of these in *years*."

"It's a police radio," he said, "not a toy. If there's an emergency, you can reach me by using channel eleven and pushing this button here to talk." He reached over and showed her.

"An emergency? You think there's going to be an emergency?"

"No, I don't. This is just in case. Better safe than sorry. Besides, you were complaining about not having a phone in your room, and considering the propensity you city folks have for calling the police every time someone sneezes after midnight, I figured this would make you feel better. Safer."

In other words, she thought with a private smile, he cared about her but he didn't want to admit it.

"Thanks," Josie said sincerely. "That was really sweet of you."

"I'm not sweet," Dan said gruffly. "Don't go getting the wrong idea. I'm doing this as much for my own peace of mind as for yours." It was the first time Josie had seen Dan look embarrassed.

It was charming on him.

"Don't you have to go back in there?" he asked.

"Yes." Josie peered through the window. People were milling around again, clanking beer bottles and laughing. "It looks like the signing has finally broken up." That was a relief. She hadn't missed much, maybe just fifteen minutes or so. Presumably Beatrice hadn't said anything too heinous in that short amount of time. "Are you leaving?" she asked Dan.

He gave a short nod. "I'm going back to the station."

"Do you ever sleep?" she asked, then immediately regretted her choice of words. "I mean, it seems like you're working all the time."

"I sleep," he said, then added with a wicked smile, "I'd be glad to prove it, if you want to stay for a few days after the cook-off."

Josie paused. Even though he was joking, the idea of staying a little longer had its appeal. The town was growing on her rapidly. Already she was almost used to the pace. She kind of liked being able to sleep late and not feel like the rest of the world was now ten steps ahead of her. She liked the feeling of quiet that filled the thick, honeysuckle-scented air, as opposed to the constant thrum of traffic and sirens. Despite how busy she'd been, in a way she felt calmer than she'd felt in a while. Beldon was a nice place. She couldn't stay, of course, but one of these days maybe she'd come back for a vacation.

Maybe she'd even get to see the chief of police sleep then.

"Thanks for the offer," she said. "But I think I'd better get back inside."

He nodded. "Remember, channel eleven."

She glanced down at the radio. It was already set on channel eleven. "Got it," she said, waving it in the air. "Thanks."

When she went back inside, she felt giddy in a way

she couldn't recall feeling since high school. It was ridiculous, with everything she had to do and everything she had to worry about, for her to keep locking lips with the chief of police, but something about Dan Duvall was captivating.

Of course, it was clear that she wasn't the first woman to notice that. She had to keep reminding herself of that fact so she didn't get too wrapped up in the idea of a great-looking playboy who lived hundreds of miles from her and who probably wouldn't remember her name in a week.

"Ms. Ross." Buzz Dewey hurried over to Josie, a worried expression on his face. He didn't look like a man who could afford too many worries.

"Yes?" she asked, instinctively using her most soothing voice.

"I'm glad I found you." He took a moment to catch his breath. "I just wanted to let you know that Ms. Beaujold has gone to her room for the evening. I helped her there myself."

"Was she ill?" Josie asked, trying to determine the source of his obvious anxiety.

"No, no, no, indeed not. She was merely…that is, she'd had a few shots of Cutty Sark—"

"When? I was only gone for fifteen or twenty minutes."

Buzz's entire head became a pink lightbulb, and he ran a hand across his scalp. "Yes, well, that was about it, the last fifteen or twenty minutes of her book signing."

"How many shots did she have?"

Buzz swallowed. "Maybe…ten. Fif-fifteen at the outside."

Josie's breath left her in one long hiss. "So when you say you helped her upstairs, what you mean is that you carried her up."

Buzz nodded frantically. "Along with the help of several others. Very discreet folks, though." He held a shaky finger to his lips. "I'm sure they won't say a word."

Josie pinched the bridge of her nose. The headache was threatening again. "If Beatrice had ten or fifteen shots before you took her up, it probably wasn't a huge secret that she'd had too much."

"She wasn't…quiet," Buzz agreed.

Was she ever? "Don't worry about it, Mr. Dewey. I'm very glad you were there to help her. And, to tell you the truth, she's probably better off in her room than out of it at this point."

He nodded his agreement. "I don't believe she'll be out again before morning."

That was good news. In fact, that was very good news. Josie needed the sleep herself, and with Beatrice passed out in her room, that was one big worry she didn't have to think about.

Chapter Eleven

FROZEN PERSIMMON JAM
(from page 147 of *The Way to a Man's Heart*
by Beatrice Beaujold)

Spread this cool jam on a hot buttered muffin and see if things don't heat up in your relationship.

5 cups puréed persimmons
3 cups granulated sugar
1/4 cup fresh lemon juice
1 teaspoon grated orange zest
pinch ground cloves
pinch nutmeg

Combine everything in a medium saucepan and bring to a gentle boil over medium heat. Cook for 30 minutes, stirring frequently.

Pour into prepared, sterilized jars, seal and store in the freezer.

Dan went to the inn early the next morning with the intention of questioning Beatrice Beaujold's niece. He didn't know what he was going to ask her, or what, exactly, he hoped to learn by talking to her, but something about her didn't add up.

He pulled into the parking lot and got out of the car, aware of a feeling of being watched. He turned around just in time to see his brother dodge behind a tree.

He hesitated, then decided to ignore it and started walking toward the door. Gravel crunched under footsteps behind him and when he turned to look again, Jerry dodged behind a car.

Dan stopped. "Jer."

There was no answer.

"Yo, Jer. There behind the '65 Mustang."

Jerry slowly emerged, using one hand to slap gravel dust off the knees of his pants. In the other hand, he was holding an English muffin covered with red jam. "Yeah, Dan?"

"What are you doing?"

Jerry took a bite of the muffin, getting red jelly on his chin. "Eating. You should try this jam, man. The cookbook lady's niece made it. I think I could marry her if she'd make this every morning."

"I mean, why are you following me?"

"Oh. I'm tracking down a story."

"What's that got to do with me?"

"You've got the story," Jerry said, his mouth full.

"What story?"

"The cookbook lady. Someone's trying to kill her."

Dan shook his head. "No one's trying to kill her, Jer. She's just here to judge the stupid contest."

"What about all the stuff that keeps happening? The accidents, the fire, the vandalism to your car. What's that all about?"

"Jerry, you know damn well that stuff happens every year. Every single year."

Jerry sighed dramatically. "Yeah, I know. I just want to do a good story."

"Even if it's not true?"

A sneaky gleam came into Jerry's eye. "Hey, if I report the facts and it looks like someone's trying to kill that lady, it's not my fault."

"Don't do it," Dan warned. "I don't want you making my job any harder."

"All right, all right." Jerry looked up at the sky for a moment, then, just as Dan was turning to go back in, asked, "So where you going now?"

"Inside." Dan went in and took the stairs up to the top floor where Ms. Beaujold and her niece were staying.

The hallway was empty and he hesitated outside Josie's door, wondering if she was still asleep in there. And what she looked like if she was.

After a moment of speculation, he kept walking, but he had the feeling again that he was being

watched. He slowed his pace. The floor creaked behind him.

He stopped suddenly and turned, only to have Jerry
run smack into him, mushing his jelly-smeared muffin
directly into Dan's stomach. When Jerry stepped
back, a large red jelly blotch graced Dan's shirt. It
looked like he'd been shot.

"*What* are you *doing?*" he demanded.

"Aw, man, I'm sorry." Jerry dabbed at the stain
with his hand, then shrugged and licked his fingers.
"I don't think that's coming out."

"What were you doing skulking along behind me?
I already told you I don't have any story for you."

"Danny, it's my first real job, apart from the Hunka
Hunka Hamburger Hut, and I want to make a good
impression. Can't you help me out?"

Dan looked down. "You've made a hell of an impression on me."

"You oughta rinse that out right away. That stuff
can stain, believe me."

Dan doubted it would come out easily, but he
didn't want to go home and change if he didn't absolutely have to. He was the only one on duty at the
inn for the next hour because he'd let his men have
a couple of extra hours to sleep in.

"Go get some club soda," he told Jerry as he
started down the hall. "I'm going to the bathroom to
try to clean this up."

"Good plan, man." Jerry followed him around the
corner and into the bathroom.

"What are you doing, Jerry?"

"I was coming to see if the stuff comes out with water," Jerry explained.

"Go get the damn club soda!"

"Fine." Jerry left in a huff, slamming the door behind him.

Josie woke to the sounds of voices in the hall. She looked at the alarm clock on the bedside table and saw that she didn't have to get up for another half an hour. She stretched and tried to roll over and go back to sleep but the sunlight slanted right across the wall over her head. Now that she'd opened her eyes it was too bright to close them and go back to sleep.

She got out of bed and took a towel from the rack over the sink and put it under her arm. She hated sharing a bathroom with everyone else on the hall, but she had no choice. Even Beatrice's suite—two connected rooms, really—had no private bath.

She grabbed a bottle of shampoo, hoping that there wouldn't be a line for the shower.

As she entered the hall, she saw a family of four struggling out the door of their room at the end of the hall, seemingly all at once. Instinctively, Josie crossed her arms in front of her, although she was more than decent in her gown.

She was about to knock on the bathroom door, when a thin, dark-haired man strode out, slamming the door behind him. He didn't say a word as he stormed past Josie, but his platform heel caught on her nightgown and ripped it. Startled, she dropped her towel and shampoo with a loud plop, calling further attention to herself.

Time stopped. The man opened his mouth, possibly to apologize, but his eyes widened and he didn't speak. Suddenly aware of a cold draft across her entire midriff, and down her back, Josie looked down and saw that one of the thin shoulder straps had torn, making the nightgown quite a bit more revealing than she wanted. She dropped to the floor, grabbed her towel and what was left of her robe and pressed them to her chest.

"I'm sorry."

"It's okay," she said, clutching her towel to her.

He reached for the shampoo bottle on the floor. "Let me help you—"

"No!"

The mother of the family down the hall looked at them, exclaimed in apparent disgust and shuffled her husband and children back into their room.

Josie kicked the bottle away from the man, opened the bathroom door and kicked the bottle in. He said something to her, but she ignored him and followed quickly behind her shampoo, slamming the door behind her in blessed relief.

Her relief was short-lived, though. She dropped her things on the floor, locked the door securely and turned around, only to see Dan Duvall standing at the sink wearing a shirt with what appeared to be an enormous bloodstain on it.

"My God," she gasped, adrenaline surging through her. "What happened to you?" It was something to do with Beatrice, she just knew it. She hadn't taken Dan's warnings about danger seriously enough and now he'd been shot or stabbed or something because of it. He didn't deserve that. He was a nice guy, deep down. She might have been irritated with him, but she certainly didn't want him hurt.

"I'll call 911," she said, feeling the blood drain from her head. Her knees went weak with fear.

"Hold on." Dan was at her side in an instant, his hand firmly on her arm. "It's just jelly."

"What?" Now that he was so close, she could smell a sweet, fruity scent.

"On my shirt, it's just jelly. Someone ran into me with a muffin."

"Jelly?" Well, now she felt like a complete idiot. How feeble was that, seeing a guy with jelly on his shirt and nearly fainting? "I thought…" She shook her head. "Okay, I think the pressure is officially getting to me."

She half expected him to make some comment about what a ninny she was, but instead he was kind. "I'm surprised it took this long. You've really got your hands full with that woman."

Josie gave a shrug. "It's a little more challenging than I expected."

"Hell of a job you've got." He went back to the sink and dampened a washcloth to swab at the stain.

"You're going to need to soak that," Josie said. "Here, let me help. Take it off."

He took his shirt off, revealing a surprisingly muscled and well-defined torso. "So, what, hot water?" he asked, reaching for the tap.

"Cold." She put a hand on his to stop him, then pulled up the sink stopper and turned on the cold water.

He looked at her with some surprise. "You don't strike me as the kind of woman to know about stain removal."

She glanced at him before taking some of the orchid-scented liquid soap from next to the sink and rubbing it into the stain. "I know a lot of things that would probably surprise you."

He stepped back and watched her. "Do you do windows, too?"

"When pressed to, yes."

"Can you cook?"

She shook her head. "Not at all. I've tried, believe me, and I actually enjoy it, but I just don't seem to be very good at it. My mother raised a maid but not a cook." She smiled and rinsed the soap out of his shirt. The stain had all but disappeared. "But your faith in me is underwhelming."

"Don't take it personally. I just thought you were one of those ornamental city girls who could hire people to do their homemaking, but who couldn't do a lick of it themselves."

She gave the shirt a final rinse, wrung it out and handed it to him. "Well, thanks for the compliment part of that. I guess. I'm glad to see you're man enough to admit maybe you were wrong about me."

"Are you woman enough to admit maybe you're wrong about me?"

She frowned. "In what way?"

"You think I'm a player, that I run through women like disposable razors or something."

"And you don't?"

He shook his head, holding her gaze.

"Well, you would say that, wouldn't you?" She wanted to believe him, she really did. But the thing that came after believing him was falling for him, and that scared her to death. "How about I just wait and see, okay?"

He gave a pirate smile and trailed his gaze down her body. "While you're waiting, Suzy Homemaker, you might want to fix that."

She followed his gaze. Her breasts were just barely covered by the limply hanging fabric of her torn gown. Quickly, she retrieved her towel and wrapped it around herself. "I was just coming to take a shower when that guy came running out of here and ripped my nightgown." She frowned. "What was he doing in here with you, anyway?"

"Ruining my shirt with his English muffin," Dan answered, putting the wet but clean shirt back on.

"Ah." She nodded. "Isn't he the same guy they brought into the station when I was leaving?"

A muscle in Dan's jaw ticked. "He's a lot of trouble."

"I see." She looked at his bare chest as he was buttoning the shirt, then caught herself and looked back up.

"I'll leave you to your shower," Dan said, but just as he reached for the doorknob, a voice on the other side called, "Hal, did you remember the camera?"

He pulled his hand back and glanced at Josie.

"All right, all right," a man answered from down the hall. Josie thought it must be the people she'd seen on her way in.

"Mom, I need to go to the bathroom," a boy whined from what sounded like an inch and a half away from the door.

"You better wait until the children are gone," she whispered to Dan.

"Yeah."

Her eyes met his and held. His expression spoke volumes, but in a language that she couldn't understand.

The mother knocked on the door. "Is someone in there?"

Dan pointed to Josie.

"Yes," she called.

"Mom," the boy repeated. "I need to go."

"I do, too," the other child said.

Dan and Josie's bare arms touched as they both leaned forward to hear what was being said.

"I told you to go before we left," the mother said.

Josie's fingers brushed Dan's.

"I couldn't," one of the boys pleaded.

Josie moved a little bit closer. Her shoulder grazed Dan's chest. It sent a frisson of electricity through her.

"Me, neither," the other child bellowed.

Dan's arm bumped the terry cloth of her towel. Josie's breath caught in her chest.

"Oh, all right," the mother said. "Hal!"

The man's voice was closer now. "Yes," he said wearily. His feet pounded on the hall floor. "What's the matter now?"

"The boys need to go peetles." She knocked on the door again. "Are you going to be long?" the woman asked impatiently.

What a question. "I'm going to take a shower," Josie answered.

"Oh."

"Mom, is that the naked lady we saw earlier?"

Josie's face warmed and she felt Dan look at her.

"I don't know, Benji. Let's go back to the room."

"But, Mom…"

"Go!" the woman rasped.

Their footsteps faded down the hall.

"Seems you've gained some notoriety for yourself, as well as your client," Dan commented.

"Very funny." Josie narrowed her eyes at him. "What are we going to do?"

"I thought you were going to take a shower."

"I am." She looked at him askance. "But you can't go yet because I don't want them to see you leaving."

"Why not? I was just cleaning up my shirt."

"Yes, but it looks bad. You're the chief of police, for crying out loud. You can't have people think you're canoodling in the bathroom with a tourist."

"Canoodling?"

"Yes. What are those kids going to think if they see a man coming out of here when I just said I was taking a shower?"

He smiled.

"Well, even if you don't care, *I* don't want them to think that."

"Okay." He took two steps and sat down on the closed toilet. "Then it looks like I'm stuck for a little while." He gestured toward the shower. "Go right ahead. Don't let me stop you. Do you need someone to scrub your back?"

"I'm *not* showering with you in here."

"I admire your modesty as far as wanting to keep up appearances for those kids, but you don't need to be shy in front of me. Hell, I've already seen you practically naked."

"Thanks, but I think I'll keep my clothes on." She eyed him. "I guess that's not something you hear very often."

"No, but I'm guessing you say it a lot."

"Okay, that's it." She swung the door open, announcing loudly, "Thank you for checking, Chief, but I don't think there's anyone hiding in the shower stall, after all."

He looked at her incredulously and she shrugged, then looked down the hall. It was empty. "Okay, go, but hurry."

"Yes, ma'am." He stopped in front of the door and cocked his head at Josie. "Nice seeing you. Again."

Her heart tripped. "Hurry, before someone else shows up."

She watched him go, then locked the door after him and leaned back on it.

When her heart rate returned to normal, she went to the shower and turned the water on. She pushed the curtain back slowly and stepped in. It was only then that she realized she'd forgotten to take her nightgown off.

Dan Duvall was really getting to her.

Later that afternoon, after a long day of watching amateur cooks mix strange things together and call it chili, Josie ran into the thin dark-haired man again on her way to the elevator.

"Miss Reese?"

"It's Ross," she said archly. "What on earth do you want now?"

"Once again, I'm sorry about what happened earlier. It was an accident."

"Forget it." She started to go but he stopped her.

"Can I have a moment?"

"For what?"

"Press." He flashed his wallet too quickly for her to see what he was showing her. "I'm with the *Beldon Chronicle*."

The *Beldon Chronicle*. The very paper that had broken the story about Beatrice's drinking.

Was *this* the man who had written it?

Dan had said he was trouble. He wasn't kidding.

Still, maybe this was Josie's chance to try to repair

whatever damage had been done by yesterday's paper. But she'd have to be subtle. She couldn't let him know she was trying to do damage control.

"What can I do for you?" she asked, trying to sound accommodating.

"I'd like to do an interview with Ms. Beaujold. Can you help me arrange that?"

"Oh, no," Josie said quickly. That was the *last* thing she wanted to have happen. Beatrice had done an acceptable job of mingling with fans this afternoon before going up to her room for some "afternoon tea." Josie wanted to leave well enough alone.

"Ms. Beaujold doesn't do interviews," Josie said. "Except for the occasional question-and-answer forum like she has scheduled for tomorrow afternoon."

"Hmm. Then why don't you just tell me about her yourself?"

They were both silent for a moment, contemplating that.

"Well, I'll do my best," Josie said. "What do you want to know?"

"Hmm." This guy wasn't prepared for any kind of interview. "How long has Ms. Beaujold been cooking?" he asked, winking at her.

She pretended not to see the wink. "All her life. She learned from her mother."

"Her mother, you say?"

"Yes." She looked at the notepad he'd taken out, but he hadn't written a single word yet.

"Is she close to her mother?"

"Not anymore," Josie said, frowning. "Her mother is deceased. But they were close. Very close."

"She mentioned a sister." He lowered his voice dramatically. "I've heard there was very bad blood between them."

"Oh, no, nothing more than the usual sibling rivalry so many people face." Could you reasonably say that about seventy-year-old women? "I mean, it's affectionate."

"So you would say Ms. Beaujold is close to her sister."

"I'd say they're probably as close now as they've ever been."

"And she never, say, stole her sister's husband?"

Josie's heart stopped. "What are you talking about?"

"Or her clothes," he went on quickly. "Or anything else? It's not that kind of sibling rivalry?"

"No," Josie said in a steely voice. "I don't believe she did."

"But you can't say for sure?"

Josie straightened. "I'm sorry, but you seem to be leading this conversation in a very personal direction. I'm happy to answer anything you'd like to know about her cookbook, though."

The man raised his dark eyebrows. "So what you're saying is that Ms. Beaujold isn't a very nice person."

"No, she's a very nice person," Josie said emphatically. "She has legions of fans all over the country."

"What about enemies?" he asked, tearing Pandora's box open with his teeth and shaking it upside down to make sure all the contents came out. "Are there people who don't like Beatrice Beaujold?"

Josie tried to assume an expression of complete surprise. "Of course not! She's a wonderful woman." All she needed was a reporter trying to find the dark side of Beatrice Beaujold. It was like searching for the light side of the moon. "Now, if you'll excuse me I have some…things…I have to do. I've enjoyed this, Mr…?"

"Duvall. Jerry Duvall."

Duvall. Josie couldn't believe it. "As in Dan Duvall's…"

"That's right, his brother. But don't worry, I can remain objective." He winked again. Or maybe he had a nervous tick. "Might I see you later?" he asked hopefully.

"You might," Josie called, without a backward glance. Unless I see you first.

She wondered if Jerry Duvall was the one who had written the first piece in the newspaper. The byline had read "Anonymous," which gave her the idea that either the paper didn't know who wrote it or, more likely, it wasn't going to say.

It didn't make sense for Dan's brother to write something like that. After all, Dan had called it evidence. Surely he knew what his brother wrote, and surely his brother wouldn't write something that would figure into Dan's investigation.

Still, she made a mental note to ask Dan about it.

If he was giving his brother special access to his investigation, that was just plain wrong.

And there was no way she was going to let him get away with it at the expense of her career.

Chapter Twelve

BRUNCH CASSEROLE
(from page 11 of *The Way to a Man's Heart*
by Beatrice Beaujold)

If your man worked hard overnight, surprise him
with this hot sausage breakfast.

1 tube (8 oz.) refrigerated crescent rolls
1 1/2 lbs. ground hot sausage, browned and drained
2 cups mozzarella cheese
4 eggs, beaten
3/4 cup whole milk
salt and pepper, to taste

Heat the oven to 425°F and lightly grease a 9 x 13-inch
baking pan.

Lay crescent rolls flat in the bottom of the pan.

Combine remaining ingredients and pour over the crescent rolls.

Bake for 15 minutes, or until bubbling hot.

Josie took the creaky elevator up to her room and tossed her things on the bed. She wanted nothing more than to take a long, hot shower, but since she didn't want to go back to the hall bathroom, she settled instead for brushing her teeth and splashing her face at the small sink in her room. She was too exhausted to take her clothes off, put on a robe, walk to the shower and come back.

She put on her torn cotton nightgown, since it was all she had, and flopped down on the bed. The sheets were cool against her back, and the mattress was just the right balance of firm and soft. She would have fallen asleep right away if the thought of Dan Duvall hadn't come into her mind, making her adrenaline surge as if a trumpeter had blown reveille in her ear.

She looked at the two-way radio he'd given her. It was for emergencies, he'd said. Did he really expect there to be an emergency? He'd said he believed Beatrice was behind all of her own mishaps, so surely he didn't think she was really a threat to herself or anyone else.

Josie took the radio in her hand and looked at it. She and her friends used to have so much fun playing with walkie-talkies when they were little. Smiling, she flipped on the switch. The radio flared to static life. It was a familiar sound.

Slowly she turned the dial, stopping to rest on various channels for a few moments at a time.

"…got just a hell of a mess over here at the Piggly Wiggly. Bring the buckets and the big mop, repeat, the *big* mop."

"…break one-nine for a ten-thirty-six…"

"…so what do you look like, Sailor Angel? Go ahead."

"…there's a code seventeen-A at the corner of Main and Harrison. Who's out there? Go ahead."

The voice was Dan's. Josie's heart leapt.

"This is Randall, I'm here, Chief. Got it covered. Go ahead."

"Was anyone hurt? Go ahead." Dan's voice was tense. Clearly when it came to business, he took things very seriously.

Josie's grip on the radio tightened. She hoped nothing horrible had happened. Beldon was so tranquil and sweet she couldn't imagine tragedy here.

"Bruised arm, couple of scrapes here and there," Randall replied. "Not too bad. Go ahead."

"All right, Randall. Do the breathalyzer and the usual. Go ahead."

"Ten-four. You want me after that, you can find me over at the Keg and Cork. I need a break after today. Over and out."

There was silence for a moment and Josie wondered where Dan had gone. She was tempted to push the button and ask if he was still there, but she didn't.

These radios were for official business, not just people who were bored because they were staying in an inn with no television or telephone.

She moved to put the radio back on the bedside table, but it slipped from her grasp. In catching it, she accidentally hit the talk button at the same moment she gave a startled exclamation.

"Is someone there?" Dan asked.

Josie scrambled to pick up the radio and pushed the button. "It's just me. Josie Ross."

"Is something wrong?" he asked quickly.

"No, I was just...I was eavesdropping on you and then I dropped the radio and accidentally cut in."

"Can't get enough of me, huh?"

She rolled her eyes, even though he couldn't see. "I was bored, that's all. Don't take it personally."

"Wait—switch to channel twenty-two. I'll meet you there."

She examined the radio and switched it to the new channel, then turned off the light and lay back against the pillows in the dark.

"You there?" Dan asked.

She smiled and pushed the button. "Who wants to know?"

"This is the chief of police, ma'am. I'm afraid you're legally obliged to answer my questions."

She laughed. "Or else what?"

"I may have to haul you down to the station for questioning."

"Then you'd better be ready to answer a question or two yourself."

"Such as?"

She thought a moment before pushing the button down again. Heart pounding, she said, "Such as where do you keep your, ah, gun at night?"

There was a hesitation before a brief burst of static, then Dan said, "My gun, huh?"

"Yes, it's one of those eternal questions." She curled up under the covers and smiled into the darkness. This was fun. "Like what Scotsmen wear under their kilts, or whether Santa Claus sleeps with his beard over or under the covers."

"You're welcome to come on over and find out. Hell, I'll even make you breakfast afterward."

"Thanks, but I already have breakfast plans. Myrtle is making huge amounts of Beatrice's brunch casserole. I'm expecting it to cause an orgy."

"I've seen the people who are going to be eating breakfast there," Dan said. "You're better off coming here and eating my bacon and eggs."

"I bet you say that to all the girls."

"Just the pretty ones."

"I never know if you're complimenting me or insulting me."

"You just need to get to know me better."

At this moment, she was willing to get to know him a *lot* better. She was beginning to think maybe she had been wrong about him. Maybe he was a great guy who just happened to be fantastic-looking. Maybe she'd been unfairly prejudiced against him because of his looks.

She had a pretty good vision of him now, lying

naked in bed, his gun on his bedside table, ready to protect his home and family at a moment's notice. She could well imagine finding out for herself.

She tapped the button down. "Then again, maybe we should appreciate life's great mysteries a little more."

"Like what's going on with Beatrice Beaujold?"

Now there was a splash of cold water. But a necessary one. "No, that's a question I'd *like* to have answered."

"I thought you wanted this kept as quiet as possible."

"I do," she admitted. "But if Beatrice is in actual danger, I want her protected, of course."

"What if you're in danger?"

"I'm not. Nothing's happened to me." She reached up and knocked on the wooden headboard. "Besides, I hear the police in this town are working around the clock to protect innocents like me."

He pushed the button and simply scoffed at her.

After a moment, she pushed the button again. "I'd ask what you mean by that, but I'm afraid you'd answer." She rolled over and put her free hand on the soft pillowcase, imagining him there. It was crazy, yet she was kind of enjoying the thrill of flirting for the first time in years. Probably since high school.

"I'm serious, you know," he said. "Hopefully what we've been seeing are a bunch of pranks, but I'm not positive about it. Strange thing, though. Witnesses reported seeing Ms. Beaujold in the display room just before the fire started."

"That's ridiculous—she was in the kitchen with us."

"I know."

"So have you questioned these witnesses? Maybe those are your suspects right there. Who were they?"

"Buffy Singer was one of them."

Buffy. Was there something strange going on with her or was it simply a matter of this being a small town? Josie couldn't believe Buffy had bad intentions. "Well, she must be mistaken."

"You can't think of any reason Ms. Singer or anyone else might want to hurt Ms. Beaujold?"

"Chief Duvall, I can't think of someone who *doesn't.*" She laughed.

He chuckled, too. "How about someone who wants it badly enough to act on it?"

"That I don't know. I mean, she's a cranky old thing, but I don't think she really *means* anyone harm."

"Well, someone might mean her harm, and with you by her side all the time, I'd like you to be careful, too. Just keep your eyes open."

"Yes, sir."

"Call me if you have any concerns at all."

"Ooh, so I get to keep the walkie-talkie?"

"It's a two-way radio, and yes, you can keep it for as long as you're here." There was static for a moment, and Dan's voice was lost.

"What?" Josie asked, straining to hear.

"I've got a call," Dan said, sounding irritated. So maybe he was enjoying this, as well. "Get some sleep."

"I will." She lifted her thumb from the button, then pushed it again. "Thanks."

His answer, if he gave one, was lost in a sea of static. The moment was over.

Dan couldn't stop thinking about Josie the rest of the night. Every time a call came in—and they were frequent—he hoped it was her. Not calling because there was something wrong, but because she wanted to give him more grief. He was starting to enjoy that from her.

Instead, though, he just took the usual series of calls: two Peeping Toms, four noise complaints and, as usual, a naked motorcyclist in the town square.

By the time Dan got home, he was more exhausted than he could ever remember being before. His head had no sooner hit the pillow than he was out.

And dreaming.

About a woman.

Her face was turned away and he put his hand on her shoulder. "I've been waiting for you for so long," he heard himself say.

She looked up. It was…it was Josephine Ross. She smiled and his heart tripped. "I've been waiting, too," she said in that melodious voice.

"What took you so long to come to me?" she asked him. Her luminescent eyes were fixed on him.

"I didn't trust you." He shrugged. "I didn't trust my feelings for you."

"Why?"

He hesitated, then let out a long breath. "The one

time I thought I was in love, it didn't work out. She was from the city and hated everything to do with Beldon, even though she said she loved me. But when my father died and I had to come back and take care of things here, she was gone. Whatever love meant to her, it didn't mean the same thing it meant to me.''

Her eyes filled with sympathy. ''I'm not her. I'm not like her. Do you trust me now?''

''Yes.'' He took her into his arms. She was warm, and fit perfectly against his body. ''You're not like anyone I've ever met.'' He kissed her cheek. She smelled like spring flowers, damp from rain.

''I want to make you happy,'' she murmured.

''You could,'' he said. ''I believe you could. Except…''

''Shh.'' She laid a slender finger on his lips. ''No exceptions. There are no problems for us. Nothing matters now except us being together, building a life together.''

He bent to kiss her. In an instant she was in his arms, and they melted into a hot, liquid kiss.

It was the culmination of a lifetime's desire. Dan had never been so sure of anything in his life. This was *right*. He would walk through fire for her, he would do anything just to be able to keep her next to him forever. Maybe they'd even have a couple of kids.

She pulled gently from his embrace. ''I love you.''

''I love you, too,'' he said, letting out a breath that he seemed to have been holding for years. It had never felt so good to say that.

She brushed her finger across his cheek. "We'll name our first son Daniel."

Dan's heart pounded. "Are you sure?"

She nodded. God, she was beautiful. Then suddenly her voice changed slightly. "Yeah, man. He's here now. He's asleep."

He frowned. Something wasn't right. "What did you say? He's here now?"

"Yeah, he's going to be pissed," she said, but as she spoke she began to disappear. "Let me handle it." It didn't sound like Josie's voice anymore—it was a man's voice, a familiar one, but he couldn't quite identify it.

Suddenly, Josie was gone. Vanished, into thin air.

Dan opened his eyes to the glare of his bedside lamp. It had all been a dream. A dream about Josie Ross.

Now, that was disconcerting.

"Yeah, I'll let him know." It was Jerry talking.

Dan looked around groggily. At the desk, an uncharacteristically somber Jerry was on the phone.

"Uh-huh. Yeah, I'll tell him. Right. Later." He hung the phone up with a decisive click, then turned to Dan. "Hey, how're you doin'?"

"What's going on?"

"Sit down, man. I've got something to tell you."

"I *am* sitting down. I'm in *bed,* for God's sake, Jer. What's wrong?"

"Randall's been shot."

Chapter Thirteen

PIE APPLES
(from page 67 of *The Way to a Man's Heart*
by Beatrice Beaujold)

My mama always called these "pie apples" and said no red-blooded man could resist them. You can serve them any time of the day or night, with any meal or on their own.

1/4 cup butter
4 large Granny Smith apples, peeled, cored and sliced 1/4-inch thick
2 teaspoons cornstarch
1/4 cup water
1/2 cup light brown sugar

1 teaspoon ground cinnamon
¹/₄ teaspoon nutmeg

Melt the butter in a large pan and add the apples. Cook over medium heat, stirring constantly, until the apples are tender-crisp, about 5 minutes.

Dissolve the cornstarch in the water and pour it into the pan. Stir.

Add brown sugar, cinnamon and nutmeg, raise heat to boil for 2 minutes, then serve.

Dan sat bolt upright. "What?"

"Randall was shot." Jerry nodded. "Over at the Keg and Cork."

Dan sprang from bed, muttering obscenities about the cook-off. "Where is he?"

"He's at the hospital."

"Do they know anything yet?"

"They know it was a bloody mess."

Dan's jaw tightened. "Is he going to be all right?"

"He's going to live. But he may have trouble doing this." Jerry shrugged.

"Doing what?"

"This." Jerry shrugged again.

"Shrugging?"

Jerry pointed a finger gun at him. "Bingo." He looked at his finger, then drew it back, shoving his hands into his front pockets.

Dan took a breath and counted to three. "Jerry, are you saying, in your own convoluted way, that Randall was shot in the shoulder?"

"Well, yeah. It was just a flesh wound. What did you think I was saying?"

Dan sat back on the bed, his shoulders sagging in relief. "You know, you could have mentioned that part right up front. Jeez, you had me thinking he was lying in the emergency room fighting for his life."

"I didn't say that."

Dan shook his head and stood up again, pounding around his room looking for clothes. "Did anyone see what happened?"

"Couple of people. The bar was closing so there weren't many people there."

"Anyone able to ID the perp?" Dan pulled his jeans on.

"Oh, yeah. You're going to love this."

Dan pulled a T-shirt over his head. "I already hate it. Who was it?"

"That cookbook lady." Jerry laughed. "Can you believe it?"

Dan's heart stopped dead in his chest. "What cookbook lady?"

Jerry rolled his eyes as if he were talking to an idiot. "The one who wrote the cookbook. Beatrice Bouvier."

"Beaujold." Well, at least it wasn't Josie. Not that he'd thought it was.

But this was definitely going to cause some serious problems for Josie.

"Where is she now?"

"Down at the station. Hunter called here, but your phone was off the hook so he called me."

"My phone isn't off the hook." He looked at the bedside table, where he'd put his gun when he'd gone to bed. Sure enough, the receiver had been knocked out of its cradle. He was so tired he hadn't even heard it.

"Told you."

"Have they booked her?"

"Locked her up." Jerry smiled. "You want me to go tell her PR person?" He wiggled his eyebrows. "I wouldn't mind the chance to see her at this hour."

"No!" Dan barked.

Jerry shrank back. "Okay, okay, I just thought I'd help you out. Naturally I'll be writing a story about this, but it's too late to get it in tomorrow's paper so I don't have to turn it in until tomorrow night."

Dan went to Jerry and grabbed him by the wrist just as he was turning for the door. "You do not write a word about this, do you understand?"

"Yeah, right, Danny," he scoffed. "Scoop of my life, and you don't want me to write about it."

Dan held fast to his wrist. "I'm serious, Jer. You write one single word and I'll have you arrested for interfering with a police investigation."

"You wouldn't."

"No?"

Jerry paled a shade. "Aw, man, you would, wouldn't you."

"Damn straight I would." He let go of Jerry. "Which reminds me, are you the anonymous reporter who put that thing about her in yesterday's paper?"

"What thing?" Jerry looked blank.

"About Ms. Beaujold getting drunk at some Renaissance Festival and getting stuck in someone's armor."

Jerry's face remained expressionless. "Never heard about it."

Dan frowned. "Are you sure about that?"

"I think I know what I wrote and didn't write."

This was pointless. Dan had had this kind of conversation with Jerry before and it never went anywhere productive. He'd question him on it later. It didn't matter much. The important thing was that he wasn't going to write anything about Beatrice's arrest.

Not that Dan cared if it got into the paper. He'd just as soon have everyone know there were consequences to their reckless actions during the cook-off.

He just didn't want his brother to be the one to break the story that lost Josie's job for her.

"Just *what* is going on here?" Josie demanded as she slammed into the police station the next morning.

"I was just having some coffee," Dan said calmly, holding a box from Dixie Doughnuts out to her. "Care for one?"

"Chief Duvall," she said, with deliberate formality. "I got a message from you at the inn saying that Beatrice Beaujold was here." She lowered her voice and rasped, "In *jail*."

"Yes, she is."

"Why?"

"Because she shot an officer of the law. And we don't take too kindly to that around here."

The blood drained from Josie's face, but she didn't answer right away. She groped for the chair opposite his desk and lowered herself unsteadily into it. "Oh, no," she breathed.

Dan raised an eyebrow. "You don't seem surprised."

She looked up quickly. "Of course I'm surprised!"

No, she wasn't. It was obvious. And the fact that she was lying to him irked him more than anything. "Ms. Ross, did you know that Ms. Beaujold was in possession of a firearm?"

Josie swallowed. Another major sign of dishonesty. Or desire. In this case, though, he was pretty sure it was dishonesty. "No," she answered after a moment. It sounded more like a question than an answer.

"Were you aware that last night, when you told me she was passed out in her room, she was, in fact, in a bar downtown waving that firearm around and threatening people?"

"No, I didn't know," Josie said earnestly. "I really didn't know. I was *sure* she was in her room. In fact, I even peeked in on her and she was out cold. I had no idea she'd gotten up and gone out."

"That's good." He knew his voice sounded cold. Josie Ross was now a potential accessory to a crime. A few hours ago, she'd been…well, something else. "Because if you did know," he continued, "and you failed to mention it, you could be considered an accessory."

"To what?" Suddenly she looked horrified. "Is the

officer...? Is he...?'' She didn't finish her question but looked at Dan wide-eyed, practically trembling.

"Dead?"

She nodded too fast. She was really scared.

"No."

Her shoulders sagged. Two spots of color came back into her cheeks. "Is he badly injured?"

"It was a bloody mess."

Josie winced.

"But he's going to be all right." Damn. He couldn't stifle the impulse to reassure her, even as fury at her potential involvement churned in his stomach.

When he'd told her Beatrice had shot someone, she hadn't looked shocked. She hadn't asked who, how, when or why. She'd just gone white and shaky and said *oh, no.* That wasn't shock. It was more like...like disappointment that something she perhaps *hoped* wouldn't happen, had.

For all the uncharitable thoughts Dan had formulated about Josie when they first met, he wouldn't have thought she was the kind of person to stand by silently as someone else posed a threat to society. It seemed he was wrong about her. And why did she do it? Because she wanted to look good in the public eye. She wanted her client to look good in the public eye. So she would sell more books, make more money.

It all came down to money with these city folks. Always.

They deserved to pay four bucks for a generic cola and twenty-five for a beer-can hat this weekend.

"Thank goodness he's okay," Josie said, laying her hand against her chest. "You had me scared for a minute there."

"I said he's *going* to be okay," Dan corrected, ticked off that she apparently felt she could relax now, that everything was hunky-dory. "He's still in the hospital. He's in a lot of pain." Of course, Dan didn't have this on any great authority, but it was a reasonable assumption.

"I'm sorry to hear it," Josie said, looking genuinely concerned. But Dan wasn't going to be fooled by her, even when she asked, "Do you think there's anything I can do to help him?"

"Not unless you're a doctor." He tapped a pen on the desktop.

"You know I'm not," she said, sounding impatient. "What about his family? Do they need anything? Will his salary continue while he's out of commission?"

He stopped tapping. "You offering to pay it if it's not?"

"Of course." She nodded, looking determined. "Absolutely. I'm sure that can be arranged."

He threw the pen down. "Well, that's *awfully* generous of you, but he has disability benefits. We'll take care of him."

"Good." She took a deep breath and opened her purse on her lap. "So what's the fine?"

"Fine?"

She pulled a checkbook out of her purse. "Yes. Now, I'll have to postdate this until I can get some funds in the account, but if you'll let me use your phone and fax I'm pretty sure I can have the money wired to my account today, which would mean it would be available on Monday. Will that be okay?"

So she thought she could buy her way out of this. Just write a check, pay a token fine and take her holy terror of a client back into Beldon society. That was typical.

"Put your checkbook away," Dan said evenly.

She shook her head. "No, no, I insist. It's only right that we pay the fine." She opened the checkbook and held a pen poised over the paper.

"There is no fine."

She looked up, surprised. "Really?"

"Really."

She put her checkbook back and smiled. "Well, that's great news." She stood up. "Where can I find Beatrice?"

"In the cell."

She hesitated and looked back at Dan. "But you're going to let her out, right?"

He kept his eyes steady on hers and shook his head. "Nope."

"But you just said…"

"I just said there was no fine," he injected. "Because you can't just pay a fine and go on your merry way when you shoot someone. Especially when you shoot a police officer." He was really angry. Perhaps angrier than he should have been at Josie. But, dammit, he felt betrayed by her. "You're trying to paint this sweet picture of your client as some nice little grandmother in the kitchen making apple pie, and it just isn't true."

"No, it isn't. She's not in the kitchen making *anything* because you're holding her in a cell. A seventy-something-year-old woman!"

"A danger to the public. She's staying in jail, at least until the judge can look at her case."

Josie felt like all the blood and breath had been sucked from her body. "She can't stay in jail!" she cried, verging on hysteria.

Dan was unmoved. "She can. And she is."

Josie's heart pounded and she made an effort to breathe deeply, hoping to calm her wildly escalating vitals. "No, no, this can't be. Beatrice Beaujold can't be thrown in jail." The implications were only starting to sink in. "She's here for *two more days.* People will notice!"

"She didn't seem too concerned about that when she was waving a pistol in my officer's face."

"That's because *she* isn't the one who *gets* concerned. *I* am." This was bad. This was really, really bad. "If you put her in jail, she won't be able to make her public appearances this weekend. If she can't make her public appearances…" She stopped. She had almost said *I might lose my job.* What had happened to her priorities? There was a man in the hospital, a woman in jail, and while she had every reason to care about her job, it wasn't the most important issue at this moment.

"Maybe you should have kept a better eye on her," Dan said. "I warned you."

It was absolutely true. She knew Beatrice was a liability. She'd known it from the first minute she'd laid eyes on her. She should have been watching her like a hawk last night, instead of lying in her bed indulging stupid fantasies about Dan Duvall.

"You're right," she said, though she refused to admit what had really been on her mind last night when she should have been keeping an eye on Beatrice. "This is my fault. But I promise you—I *swear* to you—that I'll keep her in my sight every minute for the rest of the weekend, if you'll please, please, *please* just let her go."

"I can't do that, Josie. She broke the law."

Josie pinched the bridge of her nose. A headache was threatening yet again. It was her body's way of dealing with stress, and over the past couple of days it had threatened more times than she could count. Funny thing was, Beldon wasn't what stressed her. It was bringing her job to Beldon that caused the problems. If she could just relax in this town, she'd love it. "So what happens now?" she asked wearily. She had to stick to business, not silly fantasies about chucking her job and becoming a Walton. "Where can I post bail?"

"You can't."

"I can't?"

He shook his head. "Not for this offense."

Suddenly it occurred to Josie that Dan was mad at

her for some reason. That this wasn't only about Beatrice. "You're doing this to punish me, aren't you?"

For a fraction of a second, his eyes flickered downward. Just long enough to make her believe that she was right, at least to some degree.

"This has nothing to do with you," he said.

She wasn't buying it. "Why would you be so mad at me?" she asked. "I thought we had…something. Sort of."

His cool blue eyes rested on hers without expression. "Tell me what that has to do with the law, and with the repercussions for someone breaking that law."

"Well, obviously I don't condone what Beatrice did," Josie said. "But I would think you could trust me enough at this point to let me take custody of her, so to speak. Obviously I don't want her out there shooting people."

"Obviously you can't stop her."

Josie was silent for a moment. She didn't know what to say. He was right—she wasn't a very good keeper for Beatrice. Maybe she couldn't have stopped her from shooting that man, even if she'd been right there when it happened.

For the first time, it occurred to her that maybe she really wasn't right for this job. Granted, they'd given her a difficult case to start with, but in just forty-eight hours, she'd not only let her client shoot someone— someone who might have been killed but for the grace of God or Beatrice's bad aim—but she'd allowed her to be put in jail.

She doubted her employers would be too impressed when they found out.

She had just one idea left. Just one possibility that might save her.

"Maybe you're right," Josie said, gazing steadily at Dan. "Maybe I'm not very good at keeping her in check. So what about you?"

"What about me?"

"Can you be hired as a bodyguard?"

Chapter Fourteen

TIKI JUICE
(from page 109 of *The Way to a Man's Heart*
by Beatrice Beaujold)

This recipe is for emergencies only. It's a very powerful love potion. Be careful who you serve it to, as it will bring out the wild man in him.

$^1/_4$ cup pineapple juice
2 tablespoons raspberry liqueur
2 tablespoons orange liqueur
2 cups champagne
2 maraschino cherries

Combine everything and pour into two cups. Drink slowly.

"Are you joking?" Dan asked.

"Not at all. I'm prepared to pay whatever you ask." She only hoped the agency would reimburse her.

He leaned back in his chair and looked at her coldly. "You do realize I already have a job."

"Yes, and I'm offering you a second one." She straightened her back. "Count yourself lucky. If Beatrice stays in jail, I might not even have one job."

"That's not my responsibility."

"No," she admitted, struggling to keep her voice strong. "It's not. I'm just asking for your help."

His voice softened, but barely. "I don't think I can help you with this."

Her eyes burned, but she refused to give in to tears of frustration. It had been years since she'd counted on a man for anything, but right now she felt as if she didn't have any choice. "You're the only one who can," she said, realizing she was exposing her vulnerability to him but unable to stop it.

"This is no longer a matter of just keeping an eye on her." Dan got up and walked over to Josie. "What's done is done. You can't go back and undo it. She shot a man." He looked down at her, then took his hand and spanned it from her shoulder to her chest. "This far from his heart."

Her heart pounded in response. "I'm sure she didn't mean to hurt him."

He removed his hand. "I don't give a damn what she meant to do at this point."

"Why not? Don't you take that into consideration when you press charges against someone?"

"Not in a case like this."

Josie sighed, exasperated. "So how long do you intend to keep her here?"

"Until Monday, when the judge can decide what to do with her."

"Surely you don't want this to turn into a media circus. I'm just trying to keep the peace of the town. Do you really want the national media here, on top of everything else?"

Dan shrugged. "Maybe the judge will let her leave. As long as she promises not to come back to town, I wouldn't have a problem with that."

"Then you're primarily worried about her posing a threat to the citizens of Beldon."

He pointed a finger at her. "Exactly."

"So if she was in public, say in front of twenty or thirty people at all times, you could feel pretty secure in the knowledge that she wouldn't pull anything." She could see he was about to disagree, so she quickly added, "Especially since you have her gun."

"I'm not confident about anything that woman might do."

"But, Dan," Josie said, trying the personal approach. "Let's be frank for a moment. Beatrice needs to go back and cook a few things tonight for tomorrow's reception. We could close off the kitchen while she cooks and you could post an armed guard on her. Ditto tomorrow during the reception when she judges the contest. Those are the two main things she needs to do—cooking tonight and judging tomorrow—and you can watch her every second while she does them. And I'll post any bail you want. Surely that's fair.'' She brought her argument in for a landing. ''Just let her fulfill her obligation to Buzz Dewey and his company and we can sort out the legalities later.''

Dan hesitated, and for a moment she thought she had him. ''No.''

Josie threw up her arms.

''She broke the law.''

''Maybe it was an accident.''

''She broke the law.'' He wasn't giving in.

Suddenly something occurred to Josie. ''Are you sure? Did she actually admit it?''

''I've got an eyewitness.''

''But did she confess? Or is this her word against that of your eyewitness?''

He leaned against his desk and crossed his arms in front of his chest. ''She denies doing anything wrong.''

''Ah-*ha!*'' Maybe this was the loophole she needed. ''So it's her word against someone else's. She needs to talk to a lawyer.''

''She refused.''

Something in Josie deflated. ''You already offered?''

''Of course I did. What kind of operation do you think I'm running here?''

She raised an eyebrow. ''I don't know.''

''Well, let me tell you. I do everything by the book. And that includes locking people up when they break the law, no matter how persuasive their representatives might be.'' He chucked his finger under Josie's chin. ''I suggest you go on back and try to figure out how to work around this problem, since I'm not letting her out.''

''If you're not letting her out, then there is no working around this problem because everyone will know about it.''

''It's a matter of public record,'' Dan agreed. ''But it's also the weekend. No one will be able to get a hold of any public records until Monday.''

A tiny flame of hope flickered in the back of Josie's mind. Maybe she could cook the dishes herself and give Beatrice credit for them, citing a headache or some other reason Beatrice might have had to retire to her room. It didn't solve the problem of what to do about Beatrice's judging tomorrow, but it would buy her some time.

''You won't tell anyone about this?'' she asked Dan.

''I won't tell a soul.''

Josie sighed. It looked like that was the best she could hope for. ''Can I go talk to her before I leave?''

''Sure.'' He pushed off the desk and led her to a small hallway in the back of the room. It led to a wider room with four old-fashioned jail cells, two on each side.

Only one was occupied.

''Hello, Beatrice,'' Josie said, walking over to the wall of bars.

Beatrice was leaning back on the small neat bed,

her arms behind her head, an open newspaper lying across her chest. ''They're not getting my appearance fee back.''

They hadn't even paid her appearance fee yet. So far Josie was the one who was out of that money. ''No one even knows you're here, Beatrice,'' she said. ''And with any luck, they won't find out.''

''No?'' Beatrice sat up and shook the newspaper. ''They seem to find everything else out. Did you see this?''

Panic lurched into Josie's chest. ''What is it?'' she asked. She could tell from here that it was the *Beldon Chronicle* Beatrice was holding out to her. ''Another story about you?''

''What, do you want me to read it to you or something? Take a look for yourself, girlie. Front page.''

Josie took the paper and was surprised to see a reproduction of Beatrice's publicity photo from her book. Already this article was getting more space than the last one.

The byline was the second thing to catch her eye. The article was written by Jerry Duvall. Josie scanned it quickly, anger growing with every word she read. The article asked if Beatrice Beaujold could be trusted to tell anyone how to have a relationship when she, herself, hadn't spoken to her own sister in years. Josie was quoted several times—out of context, of course— from the interview she'd been stupid enough to grant Jerry. But the interesting thing was that there were other quotes, from ''sources close to the hot-tempered authoress'' that said Beatrice had enemies all over the country. She was painted as a mean-spirited shrew who alienated people everywhere she went.

Which, unfortunately, was a pretty accurate description.

There was also an allusion to the torn photo of Beatrice with the word *whore* inked across it. Now, how on earth did Jerry Duvall get that confidential information if his brother really went by the book?

Maybe this breach of ethics on Dan's part would prove to be Josie's saving grace.

"Can I keep this?" she asked Beatrice.

"I'm through with it," Beatrice said, leaning back on the bed with a dismissive wave. "Think I'll just catch up on some shut-eye."

"Well, don't you worry, Beatrice, I'm going to get you out of here soon."

"Don't bother," Beatrice said through a yawn. "This is the most peace and quiet I've had in years. I should have shot a police officer years ago."

Josie leaned her forehead against the cold bars. "So you did do it?"

Beatrice opened an eye and peered at her. "What does your boyfriend say?"

"If you mean Chief Duvall, he says you did. And he's not my boyfriend."

Beatrice snorted. "Then you two are wasting some wild hormones. Couple of times I could have sworn you'd made him some of my Tiki Juice."

"Beatrice, did you do it?" Josie repeated, refusing to be swayed. "Did you shoot that man?"

Beatrice yawned again. "I'll tell you tomorrow. Now, let me get some sleep."

Josie watched her roll over on the narrow bed, effectively shutting her out. That was the end of the discussion, she realized. Beatrice *liked* the prison. And why wouldn't she? It was neat as a pin and she didn't have to cook or answer questions or anything. She could just lie around until the contest was over, then go home and cash Josie's check.

Well, not if Josie had anything to say about it. She wasn't going to let Beatrice *or* Dan take advantage of her.

She marched back out to the station house and dropped the newspaper on the desk in front of Dan.

He was on a phone call, so she waited, hands on her hips, until he hung up.

"Care to explain that?" she demanded.

"You're going to have to be more specific," he said, unperturbed.

She jammed a finger at the article, specifically the byline. "*That.* Haven't you read it yet?"

"No." He picked up the paper and looked at it.

She could tell the minute he saw his brother's name because his face darkened and his mouth set in a grim line. Also, he said his brother's name along with a description she wouldn't have uttered herself.

She gave him a couple of minutes to read the article, then said, "I'd like to know how your brother got a hold of police evidence, Chief."

"I would, too," he said, standing up.

"It must be against the law for you to feed confidential information about a suspect to the press."

He opened a drawer and took his keys out, then looked into her eyes. "I didn't tell him any of this."

She suppressed a shiver at the intensity of his gaze. "That's what you say. But there it is. Under the circumstances, I don't see how Beatrice could possibly get a fair hearing, so I demand you let her go."

She had hoped that would have him quaking in his boots, but instead he didn't even answer. He took out his two-way radio, called another officer and told him to come back to the station ASAP, then went to the door.

"Wait a minute," Josie said.

He glanced back at her. "What?"

"I want you to let Beatrice go."

"You mentioned that."

"Am I going to have to call my lawyer?" In the city that would have gotten a person's attention.

Dan just shook his head. "Honey, you can call whoever you want. Phone's right there. Just leave a quarter." He didn't wait for her to answer before he slammed out the door.

Josie stood there feeling more impotent than she'd ever felt in her life. She was a competent person, she reminded herself. Every day in the city she handled problems within minutes. Her life ran smoothly, even predictably.

Why was everything so different here?

Determined to gain control of the situation, she decided to go back to the inn and ask Myrtle if they could shut off the kitchen for "Beatrice" to cook tonight. Who would know the difference? If she followed the recipes exactly, they would be no different than if they were done by Beatrice's own hand. So it wasn't cheating. Not really.

In the meantime, at least Beatrice wouldn't be causing any more scenes. Josie would simply announce that Beatrice had retired early with a headache or something.

This could work, she told herself.

It *had* to.

This was never going to work, she thought later that night. There was no way anyone was going to think this was Beatrice's cooking. She couldn't lure a hungry fly with this mess, much less a resistant man.

It was supposed to be chili, she thought, peering into the steaming pot. It *looked* like chili, but then it was hard to throw so many things in a pot and have it *not* look like chili.

The problem was, it didn't smell like chili. It didn't really even smell like food. And she wasn't about to taste it.

Where had she gone wrong? The recipe was so straightforward. All she could think was that she'd been so distracted by Beatrice's predicament that she had added the wrong spices. And maybe she hadn't sautéed the onions for long enough. And possibly the beans needed to be soaked before they went into the pot…she'd heard about soaking beans but she'd never done it before.

One thing was certain—this would never do. There was absolutely nothing appetizing about this mess. She was going to have to dump it and start over.

She glanced at the clock. It was nearly midnight. She was tired. Myrtle had been good enough to close off the kitchen for the night so she could work in private, but she didn't think she had the energy to cook into the wee hours. Especially if the next batch came out as badly as this one had.

She went to the refrigerator and took out a cold diet cola, hoping the caffeine would perk her up.

Twenty minutes and three diet colas later, she nearly jumped out of her skin when there was a knock at the door. She looked frantically around, wondering if she could either hide the evidence of her cooking, or fabricate evidence that Beatrice was the one doing it.

But there was no time for her to act at all because the door opened and Dan Duvall stepped in.

The instant she saw him, she had a childish impulse to turn away as if she hadn't, but his eyes met hers before she had the chance. The shock of his blue gaze set her heart reeling and sent shivers down her spine and to parts beyond.

This is how women fall for the wrong man, she thought wryly, angry at her body's betrayal of her. They know all about him intellectually, but they want him, anyway. It's chemical. Almost beyond control. Last winter, while struggling with a long bout of the flu, Josie had watched talk shows all day for a solid week. She knew all about the dangers of falling for the wrong man.

It was not going to happen to her, she told herself as he walked toward her.

He was in uniform, which made him seem about twelve feet tall as he walked past the shelves of ceramic bowls and plates.

"What are you cooking?" he asked.

"My career," she answered shortly, stirring some browned onion bits on the bottom of a pan. "You're just in time to see it go up in flames."

"That what smells so bad?"

She shook her head. "What do you want, Chief?"

"I came to help you."

She stopped stirring. "Did you bring Beatrice?"

He leaned against the counter. "You know I can't do that."

She turned the burner off and carried the pan over to the sink. "Then you can't help me," she said, dumping the burned onion in with the last ones she'd tried to sauté.

He came up behind her and looked over her shoulder into the sink. "I can help you."

She turned to face him, surprised at his close proximity. "How? Can you cook?"

He gestured toward the sink. "Better than *that*."

She considered accepting his help, then thought she was better off declining. "No, thanks. I can manage."

He looked skeptical. "Are you sure?"

"Positive." She slid past him and moved several feet away to the counter, where she had her ingredients lined up and ready to prepare. It was safer over here. She could think more clearly when she wasn't close enough to feel his body heat penetrating the fabric of her clothes.

"Because, no offense, but you really look like you're in a bind."

She whirled to face him. "I am, actually. I am in a bind. And you know who put me here? *You* did."

"This is not my fault," he said. "I didn't tell your friend to go tie one on in a bar downtown and whip out a gun."

"Neither did I!"

"Well, good." He shrugged broadly. "Then it's not your fault, either. We're blameless. What's the problem?"

"The problem is that I might lose my job because of it. And while what Beatrice did obviously isn't your fault, you could be at least a *little* flexible about letting her out of jail so she can do what she's here to do."

"I told you why I can't do that."

"Yeah, you told me." She took some onions out of the net bag. She was down to her last few. It was vitally important that she didn't ruin this batch. "And, believe it or not, I understand. I just think we could work around your concerns so as not to disappoint the fans who have come to see Beatrice, and Buzz Dewey, who clearly has a lot invested in her appearance."

"And to save your job."

"Yes, and to save my job. I don't want to get fired. What's wrong with that?"

"Nothing," he said calmly. "I just can't do what you're asking me to do. I'm sorry."

She looked into his eyes. He looked utterly sincere.

They were at an impasse.

Finally, Josie turned back to the counter. "I understand," she said to the onions.

"Believe it or not, though, this is the best thing for Ms. Beaujold."

"Oh, no doubt. She can lie back and sleep this weekend, then go home and cash my check. No problem for her."

"*Your* check?"

Josie threw her hands up. "It's a long story."

Dan came up behind her again. She felt his hand on her shoulder as he turned her to face him. "If Ms. Beaujold is in danger from someone out there, she's in the safest place possible."

"I thought you said she was the one doing all that stuff."

"I said she *might* be."

"And you've changed your mind?"

He cocked his head thoughtfully. "Maybe so. I'm not a hundred percent sure of anything, but if I'm right, she's going to be safe and the person who's been trying to harm her is going to get caught."

"Who do you think it is?" Josie asked. "Is it Cher?"

He put a finger to her lips. "Let's just see what happens over the next twenty-four hours, okay?"

"I can tell you what's going to happen over the next twenty-four hours," Josie said. "I'm going to make a complete mess of Beatrice's recipes and people are going to figure out she didn't make them and then I'm going to lose my job or be moved to some sort of janitorial position in the building."

He laughed softly. "I won't let that happen."

"How are you going to prevent it?"

"You said you needed this chili put together so you could say Ms. Beaujold made it, right?"

She raised an eyebrow at him. "What I actually need is for Beatrice to make it herself."

He gave her a look.

"Okay, or to make it myself and say she did," Josie conceded.

"Then let's get to it." He took his gun holster off and laid it on the counter, along with his badge, before rolling up his sleeves. "Where's the recipe?"

"Are you serious?"

He leaned against the counter and held her gaze. "I feel somewhat responsible for what you're going through."

"Why?"

"You were right about my brother," he said.

"He's the one who's been writing the stories about Beatrice in the *Chronicle?*"

Dan nodded. "I didn't give him any information, of course, but he's always been pretty slick. He can get into trouble ten times in the morning before most people roll out of bed. Seems that on one of those mornings, he came across this." He pulled a folded paper out of his back pocket and handed it to Josie.

Chapter Fifteen

SLOW COOKED SOUTHERN CHILI
(from page 65 of *The Way to a Man's Heart*
by Beatrice Beaujold)

Down South, we like to take things slow. Slow cooking this recipe makes for meat that will melt in your mouth.

4 lbs. top sirloin beef, cut into 1-inch cubes
2 large green peppers, diced
4 stalks of celery, sliced
2 large red onions, chopped
2 jalapeño peppers, seeded and minced
2 small cans mild green chilies
2 28-oz. cans stewed tomatoes
8 cloves garlic, minced

$^1/_2$ cup tomato juice
2 cans beef broth
2 tablespoons Worcestershire sauce
4 tablespoons chili powder
1 tablespoon sugar
2 teaspoons ground cumin
salt and pepper, to taste
pinto beans, cooked
Monterey Jack cheese, grated
sweet onions, sliced

Combine beef, green peppers, celery, onions, jalapeño peppers, green chilies, stewed tomatoes and minced garlic in a large oven-proof roasting pan. Toss to combine.

Combine remaining ingredients in a blender, mix thoroughly and pour over other ingredients in the roasting pan.

Bake at 250°F for 6 to 8 hours. Serve pinto beans, grated Monterey Jack cheese and raw sweet onions on the side.

Frowning, Josie took the grass-stained sheets from Dan and opened them up. It was the letter from Beatrice's editor. In only about forty-five seconds of reading she spotted at least five of the quotes that Jerry had attributed to "sources close to the author" in this morning's article.

"Was he the one who stole my bags?" Josie asked in disbelief.

Dan shook his head. "No way. He just lucked into

that and saw an opportunity to make money by writing about Ms. Beaujold for the newspaper.''

''Did anyone else see this?'' Josie was almost afraid to ask.

''No. He didn't want the newspaper editor to know how flimsy his source was, so he kept it secret.''

Josie held the letter against her chest and took a deep, relieved breath. ''And he didn't make a copy?''

''He wouldn't know *how* to make a copy,'' Dan said with a smile, then added, ''No, he didn't.''

Josie took a moment to soak it all in, then went to a drawer she'd been looking in earlier for a can opener, took out a box of matches and carried them and the letter over to the sink.

She stopped and turned back to Dan. ''You're not going to arrest me for arson, are you?''

He shook his head.

''Good.'' She turned back to the sink, took a match out and struck it, then held the papers while they burned. When there was only a small corner left, she turned on the faucet and extinguished the fire, leaving just a muddy film of wet ash in the stainless-steel sink.

''Ready to cook?'' Dan asked.

''As ready as I'll ever be.''

Josie opened Beatrice's cookbook to the recipe she was making and asked, ''What's the difference between limp and transparent?''

He gave her a wicked grin. ''Is this a joke?''

She sighed and shook her head. ''I mean as it pertains to onions.''

"You do have a lot to learn."

"Tell me about it."

He took two onions out of her bag. "Peel these." He thrust them at her, then paused, looking at her earnestly. "Can you do that?"

"Yes, I can peel onions," she said impatiently, pulling a bread knife from the knife sheath. "I'm not completely useless."

He nodded toward the knife. "You might want to use something...else," he said. "Something shorter, and not serrated. Try a paring knife."

"Paring knife," she repeated, looking over her choices. She started to pull the butcher's knife out, caught Dan's subtle shake of the head, then picked the paring knife. She raised it to him. "Paring knife?"

"Well done."

He caught her double-glance back at him before she went back to peeling, and he smiled. This was one woman who was really used to protecting herself; she was leery of absolutely everything.

He pulled a head of garlic out of her bag, set it on the counter and pounded it once with his fist.

"What are you doing?" Josie asked, startled.

"I need to chop up some cloves of garlic," he said, then looked at the layers and layers of onion on the counter next to her. "What are you doing?"

She colored. "I'm peeling the onion." She followed his gaze to the counter then met his eyes. "Aren't I?"

"I'd say so."

She swallowed. "I'm never quite sure where to stop."

He put the garlic down and walked over to her. What she held in her hand was about one-fifth of the onion's original size. "When do you usually stop?" he asked, careful not to smile.

"When there are no more layers of skin."

Dan scanned the onion on the counter and picked up the papery-thin outer skin. "This is the skin," he said. He gestured toward the rest of her peelings. "That is the onion."

She looked truly surprised. "Really?"

He considered what her chili would taste like with the two tablespoons of onion she would have put in if he hadn't stopped her. "I have a feeling you're going to learn a lot of surprising things tonight." It was as though he were teaching an alien about earthly culture. "As unbelievable as that might sound, you're going to have to believe me."

They spent the next forty-five minutes discussing basic techniques and equipment. Josie was a quick study and took it all very seriously. He could tell that she had given in entirely to trusting him.

They found a bottle of cheap Chianti in the back of the pantry and opened it, vowing to pay the management in the morning.

By the time they were ready to get back to the cooking, it was nearly dawn.

"Do you remember how I told you to peel the garlic?" he asked Josie.

"Garlic, garlic." She picked up the bag of pinto beans. "Is this garlic?"

He opened his mouth to respond but she cut him off. "I'm only joking, Dan. I do know the difference between garlic and a bag that reads pinto beans on it. But these should be soaking, shouldn't they?"

"They should, actually," he said, surprised.

Josie took a pan out from one of the shelves and filled it halfway with water. Then she poured the dry beans in and set it over low heat.

"I'm impressed," Dan said.

Josie shot him a look. "I was reading up on this business just tonight." She took a couple of cloves from the broken head of garlic. "Now, I take a large straight knife—" she pulled it from the knife holder "—chop off the end," she did so, then pressed the flat side of the knife to the clove and gave a sharp push "—and, voilà!" She pulled the peeled clove from its broken skin. "I did it!"

He moved behind her and said, "Now do another one."

Silently, she repeated the procedure, but by the third time her movements had slowed considerably and she was leaning subtly against Dan's chest.

His heart hammered against his ribs. It was getting more and more difficult to concentrate on cooking. In fact, the longer he stayed with Josie, the less important the cooking seemed to be.

The heat from Dan's body penetrated her shirt and she instinctively moved toward him. "How am I doing, Chief?'' she asked, wrestling the skin off a particularly stubborn clove.

"Amazing."

"Is this right?"

"This way." He reached his arms around either side of her and gently placed his hand over hers on the knife. "You just—" he ran the blade back in one small, swift motion "—slit it like this." The garlic was done, but he left his arms around her, closing them in front.

"Josie," he said, bending down and nuzzling her neck. "We're headed for trouble again."

"I hope so." She relaxed against him.

His tongue touched her throat and she sighed.

"The stove isn't the only thing in here that's getting hot." He ran his hands up her rib cage and cupped her breasts.

"Tell me about it." She wished the cotton blouse wasn't between her skin and his.

He turned her gently. Their eyes met, then he lowered his mouth onto hers.

The kiss was excruciatingly delicious. Slowly she leaned into him, deepening the passion. His mouth was tender, yet demanding. She opened her mouth, and he ran his tongue along her teeth. Unhurried, their tongues met and moved against each other.

The core of Josie's womanhood began to tingle and she knew that if this went on much longer, she wouldn't be able to stop.

She didn't *want* to stop.

Dan sensed her hunger, and his kisses became more insistent.

When she thought she couldn't take any more, his strong hands moved slowly down her sides and hips to pull her pelvis against his. His hardened manhood pressed pleasurably against her.

"This is crazy," she said.

"Let's analyze it later," he replied, then ran his tongue down her jaw to her neck. "For now..." His voice trailed off and was lost in kisses.

He eased her onto the floor and lay beside her, pulling her so close she felt like a rag doll in his arms.

The tingle between her legs increased until it reached a point near desperation. He placed his hand against her abdomen, then trailed it down toward the source of her desire. He slipped his hand down the front of her pants. Her muscles tightened in anticipation. After resting a moment with his hand solidly against her abdomen, he moved his hand down, teasing her with small movements and suggestions of larger things.

"We shouldn't do this," she breathed.

"You want to stop?" he asked, pulling the thin elastic of her underwear aside.

"No...but what if someone comes?"

He smiled. "Someone's bound to," he said, then slipped a finger into her and instantly found that elusive spot that robbed her of her senses. His thumb rubbed firmly against the tiny bud of nerves, racking her body with shudders.

Explosions of color burst behind Josie's closed

eyelids. He seemed to know her every need. Reflexively, she turned her head and sucked a breath in through tightly clenched teeth. Her body screamed for satisfaction. Every gyration was met with the perfect motion. How could he know her so well? His rhythm increased and Josie arched her back. Her breath came out in short bursts against his hair.

She was fast approaching the cliff. Usually she wanted to savor the moment, but this time it was urgent. An ocean roared in her ears, all colors turned to red, and she felt herself approach the cliff, then sail effortlessly over.

Every cell and nerve in her body joined in a collective sigh. The breath left her lungs in a long stream. He stopped his movements and held her close. Time stood still. They might have been alone in the world. Then far, far away she could hear the hum of the refrigerator.

As Josie savored the moment, he lowered his mouth onto hers, and this time his kisses were harder, almost crushing.

She ran her fingertips across his lower back, around his narrow waist to the button fly of his jeans. The small metal studs were cold to the touch and she could feel the engraving on each one as she worked her way down. When they were all released, she slid the jeans, along with the elastic of his shorts, over his hips. Then, as slowly as she could, she let her fingers dance across his flat belly to the prize.

He moved over her and in one smooth motion, he

was inside her. She moaned with pleasure. Every nerve within her sprang back to attention.

They moved together, slowly at first, tentatively. Gradually, the intensity increased. Their motions became liquid, and Josie felt as though she would drown in pleasure.

It seemed like both an eternity and no time at all before they both climaxed, almost simultaneously, and shuddered into a long, quiet embrace.

"That was incredible," Josie said afterward. Her voice was quiet, like a distant instrument carried on the breeze.

"It was," he agreed. For once in his life, he was at a loss for words.

"Would you believe me if I said I've never done anything like that before?" Josie asked.

"No," Dan said, smiling.

She laughed and ran her hand across her face. "You cad." She looked at him seriously. "I meant that it has never felt like that before."

His chest tightened. "Not for me, either."

"What do you think it means?"

He smiled and chucked his fingers on her cheek. "I think it means I love you. And I think you love me, too, but you're afraid." He bent to kiss her. "What are you afraid of?"

She took a long breath. "Everything."

He chuckled softly. "Can you be a little more specific than that?"

She looked into his eyes. "I'm afraid of giving

away my heart and getting it back in damaged condition.''

''I would never do that to you.''

''I've heard that before.'' She smiled sadly.

''Tell me about it.''

She shrugged. ''I was engaged once. In retrospect, I can see that it was a good thing that we didn't stay together. It never would have worked, even if he hadn't been the kind of person to leave me at the altar.''

Dan was shocked. Someone left Josie at the altar? Someone was lucky enough to win her heart and then just *left her at the altar?* It defied logic.

''He didn't deserve you,'' he said, his voice quietly fierce.

She gave a quiet laugh, but her eyes gleamed with tears. ''Naturally that's what I told myself, but there's always some part deep down that thinks maybe *I* didn't deserve…well, not him, but the happiness.''

He shook his head. ''Maybe it just wasn't your time yet. Maybe it was just one of those blessings in disguise.''

She shrugged. ''If not disguise, then at least a pair of Groucho glasses.''

He smiled. ''Sometimes blessings have a sense of humor.''

She looked at him, her eyes smiling even through the tears. ''You've seen some of them yourself?''

''One very similar to yours. In fact, I didn't realize until just this weekend how fortunate I was not to have married the woman I planned to back then.''

''What happened?''

It was odd, but he felt no sense of sadness or anger, and definitely no regret. It was as if a heavy weight had been lifted off his shoulders. ''She couldn't stand what she called the 'stifling atmosphere of Beldon,' even though I had no choice but to come back here.'' He smiled. ''I've held that against city girls for a long time.''

''Ah, so *that* was it.''

He gave a sheepish smile. ''Sorry. I guess it was a good thing you were stuck here or else we might never have given each other a fair shake.''

She reached out and touched his cheek. ''So now what? Now that we've shaken, what do we do?''

For the first time in this conversation, a current of nervousness ran through him. He didn't have an answer for that. He felt shaken, all right, but he didn't know what to do with it. He wanted Josie to stay, but was it fair to ask her to give up her life in New York?

Could he possibly give up his life in Beldon to move there?

''I don't know.''

''What do you want from life?'' she asked.

He thought about it for a moment. ''I'd like to settle down, maybe get one of those shady places on Main, have a couple of kids and grow old with someone I adore. I know it sounds silly, but I've always had this picture of coming home to find my wife rocking the baby on the porch, maybe pregnant with another one. I never knew who she was, but I knew it was going to happen that way.''

Josie looked shocked. "Are you serious?"

"Yeah, why?"

"Because I—I had…" She shook her head. "It's too crazy." She smiled. "But I like your vision. Sounds like a good life."

"I think it would be," he said softly. Suddenly it came to him who the woman in that vision was. Who it had always been. He'd never been one to believe in premonitions or voodoo or anything like that, but he couldn't come up with a better explanation for the certainty he felt that Josie was the woman in his future. "We'll see," he said. "We'll see."

Chapter Sixteen

ROCKY TOP PRIZE-WINNING CHILI

2 lbs. lean ground beef
1 medium onion, chopped
2 cans creamed corn
2 cans tomatoes with green chilies
2 cans pinto beans
1 package taco seasoning
1 package ranch dressing powder
salt, pepper and cayenne pepper, to taste
sour cream
onions, sliced
sharp cheese, grated
tortilla chips

Brown the ground beef, then add the onion and cook until the onion is translucent. Add remaining ingredients and cook through, 20 minutes.

Serve with dishes of sour cream, raw onion, grated sharp cheese and tortilla chips.

It wasn't easy explaining Beatrice's absence the next day. Fortunately, a great many of the guests began drinking the complimentary Rocky Top beer in the late morning, and by late afternoon the atmosphere had become so loud and raucous that it was hard to keep track of anyone, much less notice who was there and who wasn't.

Josie wandered around, hoping her appearance would make people believe that Beatrice was nearby. Fortunately she didn't have to engage anyone in conversation, because all she could think about was last night and Dan. He said he loved her. He *loved* her! Everything had happened so fast, but something in her said this was right. The fact that he'd described his ideal future in almost exactly the terms she saw hers seemed like proof.

Which left her still wondering: what now? Going back to New York felt like a distant possibility, rather than an impending certainty. She didn't want to leave. A few days ago, she thought the city was the only place she could ever live. Now she felt as if leaving Beldon would be like leaving home, and she didn't want to do it.

But she'd have to, of course. Her life was still in New York. Her job. Her shoes. Maybe she and Dan could write to each other and visit each other and see if they might have a future together. Clearly he wasn't ready to jump into anything right away, and she wasn't going to push him.

She went to the kitchen to try to distract herself by seeing how the contestants were doing with their chilies.

At one cooking station, a small, frumpy woman dumped a white envelope of green powder into her pot. Josie squinted and looked closer at the box on the woman's counter. Lime Jell-O. She suppressed a shudder.

Another woman had a red box of graham crackers on her counter. Josie gathered that a lot of these contestants were finalists because of their recipes' originality, not necessarily their good flavor.

Meanwhile, people milled around, taking pictures and producing a steady hum of conversation. It was actually kind of fun, despite the strain of making up for Beatrice's absence.

Josie tried several more times to get Dan to let Beatrice out, if only for an hour so she could judge the contest, but he wouldn't budge.

It took some doing, but Josie managed to persuade the contest coordinators to make the judging private, so no one would notice Beatrice's absence. It was in everyone's best interest at this point to keep that quiet.

At one point in the afternoon, Josie saw Dan and Cher in conversation in a dark, quiet corner of the lobby and wondered if he had something on her. Then she saw him hand her something and she left, leaving Dan alone.

Josie went to him. "I gather you don't think Cher's involved in this?"

His pale gaze was sharp. "What makes you say that?"

"I saw you talking to her, but you just let her go."

He nodded without comment.

"Dan, come on. It's obvious you know something you're not telling."

"Me?"

"Yes, you."

"I know a lot of things I'm not telling you."

"Then throw me a bone, Chief. What's going on?"

He appeared thoughtful for a moment, then asked, "You ever think about moving out of the city?"

"Huh?" That was not what she was expecting from him. "What are you talking about?"

He shrugged. "Just making conversation. It seems like this job of yours is pretty stressful and I just wondered if you ever thought about, you know, leaving it all behind and finding a quieter life out there. Somewhere."

Her heart thrummed in her throat. "I don't know," she said carefully. "Have you ever thought about leaving Beldon and maybe trying out life in the big city?" Josie's stomach hit the floor.

"Did that."

She was surprised. "You did?"

He nodded. "I was a cop in D.C. for five years."

"You're kidding! Didn't you like it?"

"It was all right, but when my dad died I came back and realized how much I'd missed the laid-back atmosphere of Beldon, so I stayed."

It made sense now. "And that's when the woman you told me about last night…"

He nodded. "We parted ways at that point. Thank goodness."

"So now you're living happily ever after?"

His gaze was even. "That has yet to be seen."

She imagined yet again what it would be like to stay in Beldon herself. The blue 1930s bungalow on the corner of Main and Magnolia was for sale. Maybe she could buy it, do her work by telecommuting, maybe even get a dog. What would happen if she gave it all up to move here? Would she and Dan stay together? Or would he be horrified that a one-night stand had moved into his town?

She didn't think he'd be horrified. She also didn't think he saw her as a one-night stand. Obviously she'd been wrong about men before, but this time she had a feeling she was right.

"Excuse me, can I have your attention?" Jerry Duvall called from the doorway. He tapped a spoon against a glass but it broke in his hand. He looked at it, then set the broken glass and spoon down on a side table and went on as if nothing had happened. "Beatrice Beaujold is giving a press conference in the kitchen. Everyone is invited to come hear what she has to say."

Josie's jaw dropped. Beatrice was out of jail and

giving a *press conference?* And *Jerry Duvall* was the one announcing it? What on earth was going on?

She glanced at Dan. "You let her out?"

He shrugged, but she noticed he didn't look surprised. "Nope. Let's go see what this is about."

She didn't need to be persuaded. She pushed past the throng of drunks who were stumbling toward the kitchen. By the time she got there, Beatrice was already standing on a chair in front of the wide picture window.

"Can everyone hear me?" she bellowed.

The crowd quieted.

"There's been a lot of talk about my cookbook here this weekend and the guilt has finally gotten to me. I have to come clean and tell you all I'm a fraud."

A collective murmur rolled over the crowd.

Josie's stomach hit the floor.

"That's right, a fraud," she repeated. "I don't know nothin' about men. Hell, I had to steal my second husband from my own sister because I couldn't get my own man. That's right. Ruined both their damn lives, too."

Josie's breath caught in her chest. This was a train wreck. She knew she should do something to stop it, but how could she? It wasn't as if she could stand up on the counter and announce that Beatrice was joking. All she could do was stand by and watch her career go down the drain.

The strange thing was, it didn't bother her nearly as much as she would have expected. In fact, the most overwhelming feeling she had was one of relief. She'd placed far too much emphasis over the past few months on her job, and doing everything she could to impress everyone else, even if it meant she had to be something slightly other than herself.

It was an internal battle that had raged particularly badly over the past few days, and left her wondering if she was really doing what she wanted to with her life.

The answer was a resounding no.

Just a few days in Beldon had made her realize that a quieter life appealed to her. She liked being able to walk safely from one side of town to the other. She liked opening her window at night and hearing crickets chirping instead of sirens blaring.

She liked flirting with Dan over sweating glasses of lemonade, and she particularly liked the way it felt to be in his arms when they were alone.

He'd asked her if she ever thought about leaving the city.

She suddenly realized that she'd been thinking about it for days.

"…and furthermore, I don't even *like* men," Beatrice was saying. "I'm a scheming, cheating—"

"Don't forget lying!" a voice called from the back of the room.

Beatrice's voice!

Josie turned to see Beatrice standing in the doorway, her hands on her hips.

Doing a comical double-take, along with everyone else in the room, Josie whipped her head back to the chair in front of the window where Beatrice still stood.

"That woman is a liar!" the Beatrice in the back of the room announced, pointing toward the Beatrice in front of the window.

Josie wondered if she'd finally gone insane, or if this was some kind of bizarre dream.

"That's my sister Madge," the Beatrice in the back of the room continued. "And she's come here to try to ruin my good name."

Now things were starting to make sense. Josie looked at Dan, who was still standing beside her, smiling.

"So you *did* let her out of jail," Josie said.

He shook his head. "Technically, no. But I had Cher go down to the station and give a note to one of my men to free her."

"Cher? You had Cher working for you?"

"Only today. Until then, she was working for her aunt." He pointed to the one in front of the window. "That one. She kept her informed as to Beatrice's movements and told her Beatrice was in jail but that no one knew it so she could come here today and make an announcement as Beatrice."

Josie's head was spinning. "How on earth did you figure all of this out?"

"I just put two and two together. It helped that my brother was hanging out with Cher and coming up with all this information about Ms. Beaujold for his newspaper column."

She had to hand it to him. Even with all the evidence, she never would have dreamed that Madge was the one behind all the mishaps. "So Madge is the one who bought the crowbar? And set the fire? And shot your officer?"

He nodded. "I was wondering how it was that Beatrice kept being seen in two places at once. Like when Buffy Singer swore she saw Beatrice right before the fire started. And you said you checked on her the night Randall was shot and she was out cold."

"So you did believe me?"

"No." He smiled. "Not at first. But she finally started to talk when I gave her a couple of beers in jail. And she told me what she suspected. Sure enough, I talked to Cher and got the whole truth out of her."

"Why did Cher turn in Madge?"

"Because she didn't want to help her get Beatrice anymore. She felt bad." He paused dramatically. "It seems Beatrice is the *nice* twin."

"Good grief."

"…I've had enough of you," Beatrice said, marching through the crowd toward the front of the room, holding her small square handbag like a shield in front of her.

"You want a piece of me?" Madge asked, pointing at her chest with her thumbs. "You just try it." No sooner were the words out of her mouth than Beatrice had whacked her in the face with her handbag, knocking her heavily to the ground.

Madge, who had almost the exact same bag, picked hers up and hit Beatrice back. This went on for several surreal moments until Dan signaled to his men to break it up.

They hauled Madge off, screaming obscenities and threats, but Beatrice looked unperturbed. She simply straightened her clothes and asked, "Where's my beer?"

An hour later, the judging was finished, first prize had been awarded to a small Texan with a large Stetson hat, and easily ninety percent of the people at the inn were drunk.

"You still planning to leave tomorrow?" Dan asked Josie, after cornering her in the large, private pantry off the kitchen.

An ache grew in her chest. She didn't want to leave. As crazy as her time in Beldon had been, she didn't want it to end. "Well, my ticket was stolen along with everything else, but I think they'll issue a new one for me."

"Maybe you should stay on a little longer," he said, moving closer to her.

"What did you have in mind?"

He gave a half shrug. "There is an investigation pending. I might need you for questioning."

"Yeah?" She smiled up at him. "What do you want to ask me?"

"Actually," his voice grew serious, "there is something I want to ask you."

"It's not about cooking, I hope," she joked.

He didn't smile. She noticed, in fact, that he looked a little nervous. "I'm serious, Josie."

Josie swallowed. She knew her face had turned

scarlet. Even her ears were burning. "Okay. What—what do you want to ask me?"

"To stay." His eyes fell to the floor, but he returned his gaze to Josie. "To stay here in Beldon." He swallowed. "I'm not very good at this."

She took a short breath. "Chief Duvall, is this a proposition?"

"Worse," he said, taking her hand in his. "It's a proposal."

"Hey, what's going on in here?" Jerry demanded.

They turned to see him standing at the pantry door. "I've been looking everywhere for you."

"I'm proposing to Ms. Ross, Jer," Dan said good-naturedly. For once it seemed like he was glad to see his brother. "Could you give me a minute to get her answer?"

"Proposing?" Jerry echoed, then called out to the room, "Hey, Dan's proposing to Josie Ross."

Feet pounded across the floor like a herd of elephants.

Josie's and Dan's eyes locked, and held.

"Really?" she mouthed.

He nodded and took her hands in his.

Someone managed to shush the crowd and called, "What's the answer, Josie?"

From the corner of her eye she saw Buzz and Beatrice standing together. Buzz was beaming. Beatrice looked like she was watching a horse race and wasn't sure if her pick was going to come in with the winners.

Then the crowd receded into darkness. The room

was silent. Josie could hear nothing but her own heart pounding.

"Yes," she whispered. "I will."

His hands slipped up her arms and he pulled her to him into a tender kiss. Very far away, Josie could hear the crowd cheering, but it was nothing compared to the roar of her heart.

The last thing she heard before her delirium took over was Beatrice saying, "And it's all thanks to the recipes in my book...."

Epilogue

Josie rocked gently back and forth on the old rocker. It creaked against the floorboards of the wooden veranda, but it wouldn't wake the baby. Little Daniel slept through everything.

Just like his father.

She looked down at the tiny face and smiled. Just a month and a half old and already he looked just like his daddy. That was a good thing, Josie thought contentedly. The world couldn't have too many blue-eyed, good-hearted men.

"Hey, you two."

Josie looked up as Dan walked down the shady sidewalk toward them. She smiled.

"He asleep again?" Dan asked, approaching with a look of such pride, it made Josie's heart ache.

"Always."

"That's my boy."

"You lazy Duvall men. You never did find my briefcase."

"No, but I found out who took it. Is it my fault she threw it in the river?" He chuckled softly as he came up the steps and across the creaking veranda. "We owe Madge and Beatrice Beaujold a debt of gratitude for their shenanigans."

"Yes, we do. Which reminds me, I canceled our dinner reservations."

"Yeah?" A gleam came into his eye. "Just want to stay in, eh? Have our own private anniversary celebration?"

"Yes, but not what you think. I made dinner myself. Chili."

He laughed. "Perfect. And dessert?"

She nodded toward the picnic table, where a golden dome of cake sat on a white china plate. "It's as close as we could get to the top of our Taj Mahal wedding cake. Fiona's kept it in the freezer for a year. If we eat it tonight, it's supposed to bring us luck."

Dan leaned down and gave her a lingering kiss, before drawing back and chucking his son gently on the cheek. "I'm already the luckiest man on earth."

* * * * *

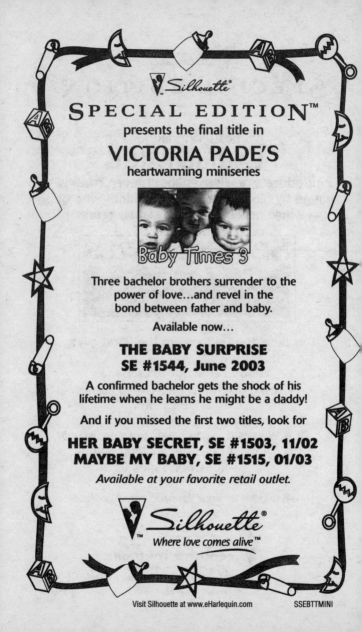

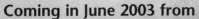

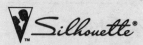

COMING NEXT MONTH

SPECIAL EDITION